Jason Johnson is the co-autho 2018) and the author of four (Liberties Press, 2015), *Sinker* (Liberties Press, 2014), *Alina* (Blackstaff Press, 2006) and *Woundlicker* (Blackstaff Press, 2005). He lives in Northern Ireland.

www.jasonjohnsonwriter.com

Did She See You?

Jason Johnson

Dalzell Press

First published in 2022 by Dalzell Press

Dalzell Press
54 Abbey Street
Bangor, N. Ireland BT20 4JB

© Jason Johnson 2022

ISBN 978-1-8380871-3-5

Cover photos by Colm Leneghan.

The moral right of Jason Johnson to be identified as the Author of this Work has been asserted in accordance with the Copyright, Designs and Patents Act, 1988.

All rights reserved. No part of this publication may be reproduced or transmitted in any form or by any means, electronic or mechanical, including photocopying, recording, or any information storage or retrieval system, without permission in writing from the publisher.

Did She See You? is a work of fiction. Names, characters, businesses, places, events, locales, and incidents are either the products of the author's imagination or used in a fictitious manner. Any resemblance to actual persons, living or dead, or actual events, is purely coincidental.

Supported by the National Lottery though the Arts Council of Northern Ireland

LOTTERY FUNDED

For my much-missed Dad, who was driven bonkers by his kids when trying to work.

Now I get it.

Jason Johnson

Miriam – One of Three

'RUN.'

Heart punches, muscles tense, fists close, vision clears.

Someone in the room just said 'run' yet there's no one here but her.

In front, a slid-open glass door to the balcony, a thin white curtain sashaying in a tiny breeze, the warm blush of a coming sunrise.

But who's behind her?

She'd fallen asleep. Can't remember much. There was a beach, sunbathing, then back to the hotel. She'd rode the lift up eleven floors. Fell asleep in this big chair.

She sees a glint in the glass now. There's movement behind. The reflection of a man by the door. He looks shiny, like his bare torso and face are wet.

Who the hell is that?

In a gravelly whisper he says, 'You persist...' and she doesn't know what it means.

Brain stampeding, her body dead still, he says, '...so I persist...' and she doesn't understand, '...and on and on we run.'

He's moving, walking closer, coming to where she's balled up on this chair.

Her eyes are fixed on the blood orange dawn and he's at the side of her face now.

And she's got nothing, no one. No knife, no hammer, no scream, no hope...

Then everything instant, everything explosive as she shoots from the chair, matched blasts from every limb, rockets forward. Eyes wide open, bare feet skidding *on tiles. And he's charging after her, the chair shoved from his path.*

But she's lightning-quick, onto the balcony and over the rail in a second, slinging herself into the whisky sky.

One

'RUN.'

NORTH coast road from Spanish Town to Montego Bay. The wheels are fast, the traffic's light and Our Trouble has just awoken, just opened those sore, burned eyes and said '*Run.*'

She's trying to blink but gives up fast. She drops those blistered lids and sinks back into the seat once more.

To my left are fences, bushes, kids, handwritten signs, ramshackle awnings, slow cats lit terracotta in the sunrise. Some of the buildings are half shops, half shacks. Some maybe half shops, half homes. Some are half wood, half concrete, half safe, half falling apart. Hard to tell where one becomes the other.

Six in the morning, sailing along here, a good driver on an open road. We're looking and zooming and chilling and no one's saying anything. I glance back at Our Trouble and hope she's returned to wherever she was.

The driver's nickname is Long Fall and I'd wondered if it's because of those gangling, noodle legs of his. But he'd said no, said he had a long fall from a rooftop one time. He'd told other drivers it could've killed him. He was messing around, he said, took a misstep, tripped over his own snaky limbs, plummeted three storeys. Long Fall walked home that night, no problem.

'In Jamaica, everyone gets a nickname,' he'd said to me, to Fiz, to Mim. 'All the taxi drivers I know, man. Everyone. Real name and nickname.'

His sharp kneecaps, blue skinny jeans, all tight to

Did She See You?

the clean black dash. He's pulled his seat forward, gifted space to the bandaged issue right behind.

Just a couple of minutes ago Long Fall was saying, 'I see a guy I haven't seen in six months? I remember his nickname. It'll be a guy I remember because of what happened to him. That's how you remember people, right? I say, *"Hey, Stuck Foot"* or *"Hey, Car Crash"* or *"Dog Bite"* or *"Crazy Wife"*. We know each other that way. I see a guy, I know his nickname, I know his story so we're already friends.'

He's started saying something else now, but I didn't catch the start of it. I miss things when Mim engages with the world. I don't hear everything when bracing for incoming trouble. The senses eat up *right now* to get ready for *what if?* She woke up and said *Run* and that's it but I'm thinking over and over *what will she do next?*

Long Fall laughs and Fiz laughs and it's about something he's said. She's in front of me, riding shotgun. She puts her head back, still laughing it up. Her black hair's catching fiery new shine from the big open sunroof, flickering and flying and sparkling and poking between the seat top and headrest. She turns to Long Fall to say something, to chat back. They're connecting easily, happily. I'm so proud of the way she does that. He's all half health and she's all full health. He's all old and she's all young. He's all stretched and wonky and crooked from the long fall and she's compact and sure-footed.

She's asking if she can call him Long Fall and he's laughing back, saying 'of course, of course,' and it's funny. He's asking for her nickname and I'm tilted left, a knee hard against the door. There's a rusty car with its bonnet yawned open. There's a thirsty dog with a muddle of big, low hanging teats. Here's a guy with no shirt and a woollen hat holding a Buzz Lightyear and looking at a bottle put upside-down on a stick in the ground and it's the most inexplicable event I've seen since I was born. Our Trouble is three feet to my right, all crunched into her door. It's as far as she can get and not far enough because I feel her presence.

The three of us laid around a couple of days back at our Spanish Town hotel. Mim went supine on a sunbed like she was trying to act normal. Fiz walked past hours later. She'd looked down, saw Mim's eyes full-on open, frying like chestnuts in a wok, like she'd been trying to stare out that big sun. Fiz screamed, shouted, 'Oh Jesus Christ No No No Mim!'

I ran over, stomach slipping, no idea what I'd see. Fiz was panicking, shaking, holding a towel over Mim's face and saying 'How long? How long? How long?'

Mim hadn't used shades, hadn't used sun cream. She was burned to shit, her skin all starting to bubble and pop. She'd gone to the bathroom, pretended to slather herself with factor fifty, poured it down the toilet. No telling how bad it is yet - her sight, her skin, any of it. She'd laid out under that sun, three or four hours, crackling, searing, burning, boiling, swelling, eyes often open on a cloudless sky. She'd have been happy knowing she was turning into some small atrocity as we were thinking we'd found peace. Our Trouble was ablaze in plain sight and we didn't see it.

We spent thirty-five hours with her tubed up in hospital, Fiz and me. We spent half of both nights on bedside chairs and half on our feet looking at the blue-black sea. We spent too long trying to avoid a small war with each other, too long pointlessly furious at the hand we'd been dealt. Among it all, Fiz's fist came flying at me in the dark like some rogue drone and Mim was turning maroon and shivering and it was all so bad. We spent two nights there as tight dressings turned red wet with breaking blisters, as forever scars formed on that sore, weak body. We tried not to say things we'd regret, things about Mim, as the medics tried to work out if she could see, if her pupils could react to any light or any dark or if they'd just been cooked.

She's wasted on painkillers now. Blind as a mole, high as a bird and happy with her work. She violated our calm and won this one. We just did not anticipate her using the sun to attack us on our one and only break. We should've considered it'd be like a new ball to play with, that she'd try to use this armed novelty against us. We could've mitigated the whole thing, made her wear shades and close her eyes and sprayed her with blocker and sat her under parasols and plopped big sun hats on top. We've been stupid and we're so tired of being stupid.

I can't think about this much more. It's so massively inconvenient, so seriously unnecessary. I need to get back to this Caribbean rest, to Long Fall and Red Stripe and Rose Hall and GoldenEye and waterfalls and jerk chicken and rum and tales of sugar and ganja and pirates and just being a tourist and One Love.

Mim's mashed herself into that door so hard now. One boiled little hand clutches her offline mobile, the other is picking at the window winder, a brittle nail digging underneath a piece of decorative chrome on the handle. Her swollen eyes are dirty purple, sideways plums in her sockets. She's mumbling those hushed little phrases to herself, those little private things she hates us hearing, her little codes over and over. She can do that whispering crap flat-out for hours at a time and never wants anyone to hear and I hope today she succeeds.

Fiz has been better at this than me in Jamaica. At home, she's been getting way worse and I've been the one handling it better. But just being on holiday has helped. This trip's been so important to Fiz. The way she is tells me she's not going to let Our Trouble screw up what's left of it.

My phone shivers, a little buzz in my palm. I'd forgotten it was there. I turn it over, look down. A message from my tough love in the front seat.

Hang for you baby x

And that's just right just now, just what I need as a new day shows itself. I send back one of a hundred nicknames I could give.

Hang for you too Shiny x

AC/DC's coming on the radio, *For Those About to Rock* and it's as good and free a sound as I've ever heard. The blistered nutcase belted into the corner is muttering more now, almost audible, mumbling faster and I just want to hear that rich patois from Long Fall upfront, to hear the compact slides and shunts of Fiz's hardy locution. Them talking together is like some clashing tonal zoo and I love it because it's like Our Trouble isn't there.

I breathe warm wind pouring in from above and some guy is waving my way for no reason. I look at a disjointed painting of Usain Bolt, a fresh mural of the Jamaican flag all hit by the new light, at big clean green graffiti saying *1962*. I want to get tangled up in the place, to go far and get wet, to grab Fiz and get lost in the mangroves, stoned on the beach. I want to get to the next hotel and make a hot little island in our room and get full of booze and lust all day before another one's gone forever.

Fiz is expressing with hands now, saying, '...but like for an adult to run, you've got to have a reason... you can run like mad when you're a kid, do y'know? Then you grow up and you've got to stop running or else people think *"what the hell's wrong with your woman? Like, where's that bollocks running to, is there an emergency?"* Do y'know? Even people who're dead fit, they can't really just, like, run where they want because of the way people'll think about it... but a wee kid can run anywhere and no one notices, do y'know...?'

And Long Fall's head is back and he's slapping one high knee and slapping the steering wheel.

He goes, 'yah... yah... yahman... it's right... it's right...' and he's loving her take on the world, loving how a reference to Mr Bolt has become this analysis.

He goes, 'Yah, I'm going to say it's okay if you want to be called Shiny. You're Shiny, I'm Long Fall.'

And she's happy with that, points a finger as if to say 'well said, my friend, well said.'

She takes a breather now and looks at hills to the left, reaches back between seats for my hand. We hold for a few seconds, squeeze fingers. It backs up that *Hang for you baby.* It says *We are strong together as we always are,* says *Everything's going to be okay.*

A girl getting braids now, some serious-looking kid fixing a bicycle tyre, some baby blue squares painted like a chessboard on a white wall. I look to the other side of the road, at the sea, at the coastline we're tracking, and Mim's broken the shiny piece right off that handle now. That shard of chrome is in her hand and she's turning it over and over. Her mouth's moving as a fingertip feels the dimensions, the smoothness, the sharp weapon it could become.

She's just broken something in this man's car, his taxi, his business. He's called Long Fall and he's the greatest guy and she's got in here all covered in creams and blood and bandages, got in here all worried about and sat on that seat and broke a piece from his taxi. And there is no way on earth I could make her know that's wrong. No point in trying. That's where the psychopath part comes in, the unbeatable indifference.

I look to the distance, at the sea's gleam, at the vast bay seen by pirates, slaves, traders, runaways. And there's a flash of metal from her hand as she's raising it into the sunlight. She's pointing it like a little knife, eyes still tight as she moves its cutting edge into the space in front and upwards to the back of Long Fall's neck. She can't see and she's pressing this nasty thing closer to him. I've got to get clear on what's happening here. My senses get sharper and I can hear her now, that random word conga, that rapid bullshit binge.

She's so quiet going, *'...sky is torn and cope when they are brief moment you persist and hang for you shiny seven hours to run and run before you go and persist live and run and let...'*

She's moving her blade closer, sliding it to where red shirt meets sable skin.

Those whispers, nimble mumbles moving faster, *'...threads about medieval insight dances in the sane with Rose Hall don't persist pretend Papillon at the crocodile waterfall run tick eight dollars and hours names are for tombstones soaked WTF persist like the wind...'*

Fiz's singing along with the band upfront now, going, *'...cos rock has got the right of way...'* and throwing her head around and she doesn't know any of this.

Did She See You?

And Mim goes, '*...run...*'

I turn to Our Trouble, my right arm lifting, knowing she'll jab hard if interrupted. She's going to do it, I'm sure. Her right hand is poised and someone's getting stuck with this thing.

But no. She's withdrawing now. I drop the arm as she retreats, pulls back her little knife, pauses that plan to stab. And she flips her burned left hand over on her knee, still gripping that dead phone. She puts the little jaggy chrome tip right on a vein in her forearm, catches a little piece of skin, tugs it up, still talking, talking, talking. She's so used to doing this, knows where the point goes, she doesn't need to look. She won't give a shit about shedding sticky blood right where she is, all over her shorts and dressings and Long Fall's seat, and that's what kills me most. She won't give a shit because she can't. It's not easy to have a kid you can't teach. It destroys you to have a kid that can't learn.

She turns to me, that thin hair blowing in the breeze. Those blistered lips are forming fast words in tiny movements and the baby bird eyes are a little open now. I see thick wet, cloudy blobs in the corners and she pulls the eyelids wider and it must hurt like hell despite the numbing drugs. Those whites are blushed red. Those pupils are uneven, sun-stained, fried. Mim's like a voodoo doll freshly possessed by some unstoppable madness.

And she quits that useless articulation, just shuts right up. Her face twitches, mouth shakes, forms some kind of awful attempted grin. She's subhuman right now, this lost girl, this recharged alien, this terrible trouble we must continue to want.

She goes, '*Run.*'

And she's beaming with that wrong look now, delighted to be holding court. We're eye to eye and that never happens. I don't know what she can see, yet I know she knows she has my attention as she's about to cut once more. Right here it's the audience and the show, the breaking and the broken, the empathetic and the psychopathic and I'd swear this makes her happy. She watches what she can of me with slashes of eyes that look burst and presses the sharpness and in it goes to the floor of a vein.

And, you know. Christ. You know? I just have to say Christ. Or damn. Whatever. I just have to say whatever. Let the wheels roll. Let the sun climb up and beat on. Let the music rule. Let new friends talk like old. Let me alone, Mim. Make your mess, Mim.

So I don't reach out.

And I don't speak.

And I don't wait to see the little blood head pop out and dash away, that dark train rolling again. Just try me today, Mim. I won't even flinch.

I close my eyes to disconnect from what's beside me. And there's the click of a seat belt -

Ah.

No.

Pelted forward.

My leg kicked. A thump at my face. Head rams into the seat in front. Rollercoaster force. Tongue bitten hard. Nose singing. Bleeding?

Ah.

Long Fall's stabbed the brakes. A hard stop on this main coastal road. We're screeching up to a startled woman with plant pots in her hands, to a frozen boy with a green shirt and breakfast at his mouth. Mim's foot's in front of me. And it's away. She's through the sunroof now, car still stopping. Her leg strikes the back window, she slips on the boot, falls on the road behind, a thud from the tarmac. I turn fast but in slow motion and my neck's weird.

She's up, running now, sprinting and bleeding and blind on the north coast road from Spanish Town to Montego Bay.

Two

Assert: Everything in your life is your fault.

I'VE wondered if she was insane at birth. You shouldn't think that about a baby, but I had my reasons. In among the insanity of normal infant behaviour, I saw something else in Mim, something more cruel than explorative, an exactness in her meanness. She'd make people unsettled fast. After just a minute or two of holding her, most wanted to be somewhere else. Parents, acting on some deep instinct, didn't like it when their kids were close. They'd lead their little ones away with cheap excuses.

I asked one of the shrinks about it one time. Mim was about six or seven, still getting diagnosed. I said if she was going to end up being formally listed as having a whole host of things adding up to insanity, which was obvious by then, did it mean she'd always been insane?

He didn't like the question. He said mental illness was developed, a combination of genetics and environment. He said it was impossible to diagnose in an infant. He said the word insane didn't enlighten anyway, that it was a legal, not medical, term.

I told him not to get me wrong, that I had nothing against the insane. I said there had been some colossal maniacs in my family history, including a woman who set out to become a war criminal and a man who ate stones. All were considered mad early on.

He shook his head a lot, said, 'Look, Mr Bic. Look. Please. There is no insane baby. There's no way to demonstrate such a thing. There's no definition, no context, no behavioural specifics to interrogate, nothing installed in there to unpack.'

To be honest, it seemed easier for him to just think I was the unhinged one in that conversation. He said it didn't matter anyway. He said it was too late to talk about insane babies in Mim's case because she was no longer a baby. But I was right. There was something constitutionally stormy within Mim's mind. She didn't learn what she became because no one teaches stuff like that. That clever nastiness was always part of who she was. When I write my story, I'll just be blunt about that and people can think what they want.

We didn't know what to call her as a baby. Fiz wanted an old name and I wanted something new. I said she was the future and Fiz said she was not yet the future. She suggested Mabel and I suggested Apple. She said Autumn and I suggested Saturn. She wanted Kerri and I wanted Derry-Londonderry. We called her Miriam so I suppose Fiz won, but that was okay. It was her baby. We called her Miriam but she got Mim most of the time. We thought it was a nice word, happy, fun. Over the years it became a loud word, often shouted, screamed. It was a word naming the source of problems, that bookended conversations about almost everything bad in our lives. Yet that was then.

What effect has it all had on me? I don't know. I used to get embarrassed, paranoid, furious, ashamed, but I got past all that. I've had the talking therapies, the long chats with caseworkers, cops, passing friends, and I can only say in the end it's probably made me stronger. Yet no one has been able to tell me that because the stronger you get the less you need so the less you reveal. Those helpful chats were winding things, open-ended conversations which didn't need a full details dump and got shorter as time went on. Truth is, not even a sleeping dog or beautiful sunset or empty bottle has got the full bhuna about life with Mim. Thinking about it now, thinking about how I'll write it all down, it feels like this is the corner I've wanted to turn. I'll be putting words in front of words, making them go somewhere, go around a new corner rather than just around and around inside my head.

I'll start the story, I think, with a broad reflection of Mim's behaviour. I'll write how it might sound strange to hear it described as steady, as balanced. I'll say her behaviour was disturbing, freaky, spiteful, vengeful, evil, planned, intelligent, systematic, horrifying, demonic and all of that, yet it was mostly consistent. You could count on it. The mornings were usually bearable, the afternoons were often testing and come the early evening, much of the time, I'd wish she was locked away or fatally ill. Pretty much every day, at least in the last two years or so, I wanted her life to end. That's my truth. If I'm going to write my book, I'll write that sometimes I hoped her heart would stop.

She took a train trip once with one of the many support groups who took brief charge of her. Half a dozen of the unhinged headed off to the seaside. While the carers were excited it might bring out a smile on her face, I can remember hoping it would be the last thing she did. I wondered what the chances were of her train crashing, or of her falling onto the track as she waited for it to arrive. Might the phone ring to say her carriage had detached and tumbled into a valley, careered into the ocean and raced fathoms deep, non-stop?

How many souls might have been lost in such a tragedy? I don't know. Lots. Yet if one of them had been Mim, well... it was perhaps for the best.

Did She See You?

I did not like those thoughts. And they were only thoughts, just entertainment of a kind. Yet that's how bad it gets. That's how low it goes. I'll invite the reader to judge those thoughts, then ask if they wouldn't have felt the same way.

So the behaviour was consistent. Consistent pressure. Constant discomfort. Consistently random. If there was a graph, some chart outlining where she was in terms of her madness as a child, it would be something close to a flat line. It was diabolical but, all things considered, it was consistent.

Then that same graph would have her reach fifteen. And just a month or so later that line would drop. It would shoot south, dive hell-bound right off that page faster than any diagnosis could follow.

She was fifteen when she put bleach in the plant water, in the milk, in the shampoo, in the gin, in her mother's perfume bottle, in her own stomach. It was then that she started pushing staples deep into the cheese, poured ground-up light bulbs into the cat food, into the mince. It was then that she took to punching us, to spitting at us daily, insulting us hourly. It was then that she leapt from a moving car on a highway in Jamaica, that she tried to combust under the sun to cause us pain. It was then that she first tried to bash my brains in.

I was coming into the kitchen and she'd tucked herself behind the door. She went for me with a hammer. She'd broken into the shed, broken into the toolbox and tucked the hammer away, sneaked it into the house. Its head swung past my ear that day, just missed braining me, maybe killing me. I'd turned, no idea what had happened, shoved her to the floor, tried to wrestle it from her. She hit me twice in the face, managed to get out into the garden, in among the trees, into the field beside. I called after her but that never worked. I went looking but she'd so many hiding places among foliage and ditches I'd have needed a metal detector.

She put her hand in boiling water and held it there. When she saw that it caused a dramatic response, she went on a mission to keep doing it. To Mim, that was worth the burning, worth the dousing, the creams, the pills, the wrapping, the swelling, the disablement, the disfigurement, the upset, the insomnia, the hospital, the screams (ours), the misery, anger, desperation, dysfunction. She'd scald herself then, when we tried to help, she'd run into the garden, climb that big oak tree, sit at the top where she'd so often sit and start muttering.

We put locks on the hob. Soon after we had to turn down the thermostat on the hot water, locked away the kettle, the iron, the straighteners, the hedge clippers, the strimmer, anything that could hurt.

Yet of all the bullshit we went through, somehow the fact that she was able to disconnect from the pain of boiling water was the most extraordinary thing.

It made me think sometimes about that old definition of insanity, about people doing the same thing again and again and expecting a different result. In Mim's case insanity was not useless, explorative repetition, but fearless, escalating persistence.

Mim had been what one shrink defined as 'a radically intelligent challenger' with a mind that would 'click into place.' They were badly wrong. By the time she was wielding that hammer, she was someone who was not just taking our lives apart, but who was a threat to those lives.

Did She See You?

I'd never seen Fiz scared before, but in those days, it really started to show. She was the toughest person I ever met, the bravest fighter I could imagine yet she'd become scared for me, for herself, scared for Mim. She was scared of where it would go, where it might end. Fiz spoke less, slept only minutes at a time, grew smaller. Her eyes got darker, energy lower, skin paler, dryer. We'd had it bad from the start but, in those months, it was like Fiz began to fade away and it was murdering me.

Mim should've had round-the-clock care by then. We could've got it if we'd been clear about what we were dealing with. We could've had a lot more help with her if we'd pressed for it, if we'd told the truth. She'd been diagnosed with a whole alphabet of issues within severe psychosis – withdrawal, hallucinations, voices. She was in and out of care centres, had a shelf of meds for us to feed her. But the experts never saw what we saw, never fully knew what we knew.

Fiz never wanted to give in or give up, never to pass her on or call time. She never wanted to hand over responsibility for that child to someone else and certainly not to the lowest bidder care system dogged by tales of abuse and torture. That same system had never demonstrated that it knew what they were dealing with when it came to Mim. So there was no point in my trying to make Fiz feel any other way. She knew the details of her mind like no one I've ever met. If I wanted to be with her, I had to travel the same road.

The alternative to caring for Mim, Fiz said once, would be for us to volunteer defeat and enter a panic room existence where we'd hide and others would handle our trouble. We were both practical people, especially Fiz. We were politically libertarian and acted like it. We owned our problems, took responsibility for what was ours, asked for nothing, put immense value on our privacy, and did not fear discomfort which followed our decisions.

Fiz would say, *'People could legally take my flesh and blood because someone says we're not fit to care for her. Are you okay with that?'*

She'd say, *'The worst insult you can receive is pitying yourself.'*

She'd say, *'No one cares about struggling people until they kill themselves.'*

She'd say, *'It's liberating when you finally understand that no one gives a fuck about your life.'*

In the end, it was us who left everyone else in their little dependence bubble. We pledged to live outside what Fiz called *'the babysat society,'* to live unafraid despite the massive inconvenience of violence inside our home. In doing just that we tapped into something right at the heart of each other and it all made sense.

We told the hospital twice how that boiled hand was an accident, that she was clumsy, grabby, hormonal, autistic, a little more psychotic than usual that day. We said it wouldn't happen again and they believed us. After that, we backed away, went online, learned how to treat burns, how to treat all types of cuts, all types of finger and toe breaks.

Even after that hammer incident - even after that, after it was clear as light that Mim might kill one or both of us, we kept her close.

On that crazy day we were blaming the hammer, blaming the lock on the shed, blaming ourselves for not building Fort Knox in that wild garden, for having a hammer in the first place. Maybe we were all a little crazy in that damp old farmer's cottage, that small stone

Did She See You?

fortress facing into the big hill where it sat. We pulled over the gate up there on the long slope, up there on the edge of the weather. We closed the door, turned the locks, buckled up and got ready for whatever winds would come.

Three

Assert: Nothing changes if nothing changes.

I BLEACHED my hair. Went from black to white. Then I did it again. Now I keep bleaching my hair. I suppose a change is as good as a rest.

Enter my dim little office and, by design, this hair is the first thing you see. I keep the lamps low, off to the side. I keep the blinds angled, the furniture dark, the walls brown, shelves black. This chemical hair is the white dot in the inkpot. Yet I feel clean under here. Clean and light and agile.

I am high value.

The clock says he's three minutes late. People walk past, shadows shading the glass square in the door. They'll be software people. Developers or coders, something like that. Most people in this rented corridor are something like that. All downloads and flashing helmet cams. Then there's me, the misanthrope with cotton hair who tells people to man up.

Four minutes late now.

He might not come.

I stretch the back, sniff, run a tongue over newly flossed teeth.

I am seriously high value and I definitely believe it.

I clear the throat, say, *'Dinggggg'* right from the neck, let it rattle in the windpipe, feel the vocal cords shake. It adds clarity, they tell me. It makes the voice deeper, they say. I'll be high value and in charge as soon as he's here.

And there he is. A short shadow reading the sign - 'Denis Bic, Life Coach.'

Did She See You?

A hand rises, pauses. Then a tapping on my door, all soft and super polite.
I am a high value alpha male.
I give it a beat before speaking but he's already opened the door. I look him straight in the eye, let this small guy know he's on my turf now. And it's a small woman instead. I got that wrong.

She smiles and she's seriously symmetrical, the mirror image of herself. The hair's split right down the middle. The face, clothing, poise, all balanced. She narrows her round eyes behind big black-rimmed square glasses and pings them wide open like she's just come to life.

She says 'Hi!' like she's excited and closes the door.

I say, 'Dagny O'Reilly?'

She whispers, 'Dagny O'Reilly.' She kind of tiptoes to my desk. 'Little dark in here, don't you think?'

She is short, about twenty, with an enhanced BMI. I'm guessing South American roots. The accent? Southern California. That matt black split bob doesn't move. Black jeans too, matching slashes on each side, wedges of lower thigh flesh squeezing through. Black and white trainers. Sky blue paisley shirt. Thick black straps looping the shoulders, a neat backpack. She looks like an emoji. And she's taking it off now, that backpack. She's looking around her now and she is unexpected in this room.

She takes the seat opposite, eyes running over my bare desk. She focuses on me now, on this ghost hair, then this face. I let her work, give her a moment to calibrate her dusk vision. She's unsure about the hair. I look at hers and it's mutual. Her smart brain tells her to say nothing about it. Nine times out of ten, the power move is to say nothing. Reaction always amplifies.

I am indubitably very, very high value.

She's moved on now. She's signalling who she wants me to think she is, showing me she doesn't care for my trick hair, dismissing it from her gaze.

She says, 'So, you mind if I open the shades a little more? Or, like, do you have something wrong with your vision or something? A phobia about light or something? That's a real thing. Heliophobia. Do you have that? Heliophobia? It's dark. Right. Why do you need it to be so dark in here?'

Dagny made an appointment online a week ago, paid in full. I didn't reach out. I prefer not to engage at any level ahead of the first meeting.

Thirty seconds ago she was four minutes late. Possibly caught her breath outside, possibly spent a while telling herself she must go on in. She's booked the standard sixty minutes but, as with them all, I want her out in forty-five. I'm like a Bangkok hooker and I need her to know it.

I go, 'I like low light. Less invasive, more private. So sit down. Let's get to the point.'

'Is it?'

'Come again?'

'Less invasive? Does low light make a difference?'

'Yes,' I say, 'that's why I said so. Lighting is the difference between conversations in McDonald's and conversations in a quality restaurant. McDonald's makes you eat and go. The other makes you linger. The science is clear, Ms O'Reilly.'

She's turned her head slightly to one side, paintbrush bristle hair scraping a shoulder. It's an odd style, that parted-down-the-middle thing. Looks outdated, but what do I know? It could be a wig. Could be some new kind of headgear. I'm thinking how she looks a little nerdy, how maybe she's always preferred brainy to party, that she's too-school-for-cool.

She says, accent all US of A, 'So, by extension, you think people have better conversations with each other when they're wearing sunglasses?'

'That's different,' I say.

'Well that's okay then,' she says, shuffling her arse further back in that chair.

She goes, 'So I'm Dagny O'Reilly, as you know. I'd like you to call me Dagny. I'm not a formal person, as everyone knows.'

'I didn't know you weren't a formal person. Anyway, hello Dagny.'

'Hello Denis Bic,' she says as if this is some kind of event. 'Am I pronouncing that right? Or would you prefer the French pronunciation?'

'Your pronunciation is fine,' I say, and fire a glance to the right, to the black spikes on that one-minute-fast clock. She sees me do it. Her jaw lifts. There's a beautifully made-up double chin there. She spends time on that podgy face and it shows. Often when people sit there their skin gives off a little sheen, caught by the low light under the jawbone or around the ear. But Dagny's matt white, matt skinned, absorbing her environment. I've become mildly curious about her.

I sit forward, lay a palm on the desk, push it off to the side, sweep away dust that was never there. I am uninterested, you see. I'm clean in this place, in my place. I'm clean, clear and relaxed.

Always be the most relaxed person in the room as I am now.

I stand for traditional reasons but I should've done it thirty seconds ago. Now she's wondering why I've just stood up. From this angle, she looks frailer than she did. Seriously short arms. I'm wondering if she's disabled in some way, if her proportions are not what they might otherwise be.

She says, 'Do you want me to stand too?'

'Excuse me,' I say.

I get the scent of some teen perfume, something with a name like SERIOUSLY? or OMFG or SICK or YAY!

I break out a broken smile, say 'Good to meet you,' drop back.

She goes, 'You too, man.'

I go, 'So.'

Tick tock.

She beams, tilts her head a little, goes, 'So, yes. So, how are you?'

And there's the small talk, the bullshit, the stuff for other places. That stuff has no value here, and we're all about value here. I don't want any chat about the walls, the weather or the website. Words mean things here.

I go, 'It is considered a virtue in some places to avoid small talk. To the point, please.'

'Is that true?'

'Yes.'

'So which places are those?'

'At sea, for instance.'

'Well okay then,' she says. She nods. She gets it. Says nothing, narrows and springs those dark eyes open again. Yet no sound follows.

I go, 'Speak.'

She puts her head straight, goes, 'Were you expecting a guy? You were, weren't you? Expecting a guy?' It's making her laugh.

Did She See You?

I shrug, grin a little, say, 'Yes, I was expecting a guy. Most of my clients are guys. But if you want what I'm selling, your money's as good as any guy's.'

She says, 'I like how you didn't know Dagny's a female name. That's a nice kind of blindness, man. I respect that.'

'Thanks. I've not heard of it before. Will you get to the point please?'

'Sure. I'm all about the point. I can explain anything you're confused about, no problem. But just so you know, there's a lot of girls called Dagny out there. I know because I've asked around.'

'Okay. I honestly don't care. People call themselves all sorts of names here.'

'They do?'

'Yes. And please don't ever assume I'm lying to you.'

'Jeez. Okay Mr Bic, relax.'

'I'm relaxed. My point is clients make up names sometimes. They have their reasons.'

'Cool.'

'So?'

No one eye is bigger than the other here. No one ear is higher than the other. None of that stuff you see on everyone when you really look at them. She's either some evolutionary edit or she's been worked on. Is symmetry surgery a thing? They already do it with bottoms and breasts. Maybe they've worked their way up to faces.

She's saying, 'I want to be clear from the start.'

And we've started. I make some slight movement with my chin, encouraging more.

She clears her throat – unusual verbal traffic coming - puts her hands together, goes, 'I know you're a private person, so I want to be upfront about everything from the get-go. Is that cool?'

'Yes.' She's been reading about me. Everyone reads about me before they come here.

'Discretion,' she says.

'It's absolute.'

'What's that now?'

I take her eyes in mine, 'What's said in this room does not leave this room. And that is the end of the story.'

She goes, 'Of course.'

I go, 'Of course. But if you threaten to harm or kill anyone during any conversations we might have then I should pass it on to the person concerned. That's ethical.'

That head tilts to one side.

I say, 'But, between ourselves Dagny, in this room, in this little safe, you're free to speak as you've never spoken before. Nothing will leave this room. Even if you say very troubling things. Even if you say you want...'

Two little hands are up, palms facing me, fingers wiggling like chubby worms.

She goes, 'Wait, wait.'

I tilt my head to the side now, align to her body language, have a go at breaking down whatever confusion there is. Straight from the textbook but worth a shot.

I say, 'Look, it's simple. Think of me like a solicitor or a priest if it helps.'

She breaks away from my face, looks to the side as she drops her hands, collects her thoughts. Something catches her eye. She points at the bookshelf behind me, off to my left. There's a phone charger, a small TV, a cup, a dusty fake cactus. There's a vase, a stone from a beach, an old baseball cap of Fiz's. Some other stuff. A mix. Precious things. Junk. Miscellany. Bric-a-brac. Clutter.

She goes, 'What you got there?'

I turn, look at it all. A book on stained-glass windows, a book called *Wheel of Life*, one called *Birds of the West Indies,* one called *After the Red Pill,* an encyclopaedia of psychology, a Dale Carnegie, a Robert Greene, a Marcus Aurelius, a Donald Trump, a Fifty Cent, half a pack of envelopes with the plastic hanging off.

I turn back, 'What?'

'The white cap? *LA Dodgers*. Cool! Is it yours?'

I say, 'No.'

The team name's barely noticeable, weaved through white cotton in white thread. Dagny's got eyes like a hawk.

I drop my eyebrows, force a wrinkle between, suggest she's out-of-line for this interruption.

She shakes her head, tips it forward, clearing her mind.

'Dagny,' I say, 'if you're not comfortable, come back another time. No point being here if it's freaking you out.'

Tick tock.

I know she won't.

She looks at her knees, plans her words.

I am high value and this is going well because I am high value and winning.

She goes, 'I don't think you read my message.'

'Your message?'

She nods, runs her eyes around in a circle, follows up with a rapid cluster of exaggerated nods, nods that say, *'Yeah, my message, asshole.'*

I go, 'I'm not interested in messages. Here's where we do the talking.'

'It was a note with the booking.'

'Saying?'

'It's just because we're talking about discretion...'

'Look,' I say, interrupting, 'forget the discretion thing. I think you have me wrong, Ms Dagny O'Reilly. You can say anything in here and it won't leave this room under any circumstances. Including if you say you want to kill someone.'

'No,' she says.

'No?'

'So, I'm talking about my discretion. My discretion. As I said in the note you didn't read.'

'Your discretion?'

'I advised you of my complete discretion because I know you have concerns for your privacy.'

'Come again?'

She sighs, says, 'Whatever YOU say to ME in this room stays in this room unless and until we agree otherwise. Cool?'

She's still as a stone now and waiting for a switch to flick, a light to go on, for me to suddenly accept that things are now all flipped, that everything is backwards. I'm looking in her eyes and she's absolutely clear on this.

I look away, see shadows of two silent strangers lingering by the blurred window in the door, think how each stranger in this room is confused by the other. I am quiet for ten, eleven, twelve seconds.

I look back, go to speak -

'But,' she says, 'if YOU threaten to harm or kill ANYONE then I'm obliged to inform that person. And I really would do that because it's ethical. Cool?'

Did She See You?

I make an involuntary sound, a kind of low hum I don't remember making before.

I turn, chair on wheels, drive a few inches, tug the blinds cord, light fills the room. I twist back, return to the desk. Her eyes, suddenly blue. The hair's a deep burgundy. The smile shows perfect, snow-white symmetrical teeth. That symmetry would be absolute if it wasn't for a mark, a bruise, maybe the remains of a bruise around that right eye. Symmetrical if it wasn't for the little scar under the left eye. Both suggest physical aggression but I have to ignore it. Yet she can see me looking, knows I've clocked damage done. But...

...*tick tock.*

She sheaths those gleaming teeth.

I look down for a second, wipe more imaginary dirt from the desk.

I say, 'To be clear, Dagny, you've got the wrong end of the stick. In fact, you've got the wrong stick. You paid to come here. You're MY client.'

Maybe she's stupid.

She shakes her head slowly, two static hair halves.

She says, 'Nuh-uh. Do you know what the confusion is? I mean, you have no Facebook, no Insta, no social media at all. You have no phone number on your website. In fact, you have no email address on your website. Repeat - on your website? That's unheard of. The only way I could send you a message was by either writing you a damn letter or booking this session online. Are you not aware of how badly your system is set up? And then - and this bit is kinda funny - you don't even read the messages you do get! Your system, Mr Denis Bic, is like the worst. It's like anti-marketing. It's just insane.'

I say, 'Why are...'

'So - genuine curiosity. Do you know who I am? I mean, have you ever heard of Dagny O'Reilly?'

'No,' I say.

'I'm famous,' she says, 'right? I'm on YouTube, right? So, you know what YouTube is?'

'I have no idea who you are.'

'But you've heard of YouTube?'

'Yes. I've heard of YouTube.'

'Okay, good. Do you know what a YouTuber is?'

I don't move. I know she's going to tell me.

She says, 'A YouTuber is someone who appears on YouTube, right? Someone who has their own channel. Think of it like a presenter, right? Often someone who makes at least some of their living via the medium of YouTube videos, right? Cool?'

'Every day's a school day,' I say, and I'm about to stand, about to show her the door, say that whatever it is she's doing here is of zero interest.

That fat little hand comes out again, that palm on display. She goes, 'Don't stand just yet. Don't stand. I've paid to be here.'

And I pause, unsure if I'll stand or not.

She goes, 'I have twenty million subscribers.'

And she's waiting for me to show amazement or intrigue or applaud and none of it happens. I'm all poker face and nonplussed, all unimpressed and massively relaxed. Reactions amplify and I'm not doing that.

I am a seriously relaxed and unassailable alpha male.

'And twenty million is a lot,' she says, 'and I do all kinds of things on my channel. A lot of true-life stories. I travel, find amazing people, put them on my show.'

'What are...?'

'You have no clue who I am, and that's okay. That's cool. But a lot of people do. Like, a lot of people. So, do you have any idea how much I can change your life?'

'I'm...'

'If you'd read my message, you'd know my interest is in you discussing your child, your wife, your inspirational move into coaching. But first, we would spend time going over it. We'd get it right, make sure we both get what we need out of it. Because when we go for the actual centrepiece interview, we'll be going live.'

That perfectly fake, robotic, circular look of hers makes sense now. She's a child of the web, a trophy from the net, a genuinely functioning emoji.

'Let me stop you there,' I say. 'I'll not be doing any kind of interview with you on YouTube or anywhere else. I'll not be talking with you about my late wife or the girl who killed her.'

I am verifiably the most relaxed person in the room.

Her hand goes up once more. She holds that little shiny grasper and its cocktail sausage fingers with authority, with complete stillness. I look at it, at her.

'I get it,' she says, head shaking, sausages wriggling now. 'I wish you'd told me before I took the flight, man?'

'You flew here for this?'

'I did,' and she's taking the hand down. 'LAX to London, London to Belfast.'

'Then you...'

'Nah,' she says, chubby face suddenly one huge smile, 'I'm just messing with you. I have a lot of calls to make. Pre-arranged stuff. No problem, man. Misunderstandings happen.'

I go, 'This is not a misunderstanding.'

'Not a misunderstanding?'
'I have misunderstood nothing.'
'Okay. Whatever.'
'Maybe you assume too much because you have lots of followers on YouTube.'
'Subscribers. Twenty million.'

I see the range of that bruise now, how it surrounds that eye, how its remains are creatively concealed. I see how one ear pokes through the hair a little more than the other now. She looks suddenly ragged and there's something sad about it all.

I need to be firm here. This thing is new, I tell myself. This sentiment hunter, this brazen misery miner landing in my office is a new way for the world to pull me back to what I've been trying to escape - people wanting to talk to me because of my story. I'm not going down that road again. It's so very interesting that my wife was killed, that I saw it happen. It's really interesting to know that I do this coaching thing, that I help others toughen up, move forward from the hard past, reframe their own stories and get out of their own way. But I'm done talking about my past. Twenty million people will have to get their kicks somewhere else.

And there's that image again. That picture. That sound. Fiz's bloody body on the living room floor. Her eyes powered down. The black hole in her temple. Mim's still armed and crazy and screaming in the garden and my ears are ringing and my vision's failing. Suddenly I don't know how I'm still alive. Don't know how long I've got to live and *it's who you miss when you're busy not lonely* and I put my hands flat on the desk and shiver as I try to quiet the noise.

'Hey,' she goes, 'You okay?'

Did She See You?

Out of nowhere, as Dagny's waiting for me to say if I'm okay or not, I go, in a whisper, 'Did she see...' and stop.

She leans forward, whispers back, 'Did who see what, Denis?'

I say, quietly, firmly, 'Did you... do you not understand what being a private person means?'

She whispers, 'I think you misheard yourself.'

I say, 'What on earth gave you the idea I wanted to talk to twenty million people? You read about me, yes? You'll have watched the documentary. Yes?'

We are staring.

I go, 'What gave you the idea I'd talk to you?'

I blink, look away, all filling up and trying not to take anything personally and I must not take anything personally and I breathe in again and out again and I'm high value and I turn back, go, 'We're done here.'

She goes, 'I coach too.'

I go, 'I don't care.'

'It's part of my skill set. I talk to people, we work through things and I coach them.'

'I don't give a shit.'

She goes, another whisper, 'I tell them the head is smart, the heart is stupid. And, Denis Bic, you're thinking with your heart. You should put some damn skin in the game.'

What I'm going to say won't be pretty and she shakes her face, throws her hands at me, says, 'Now I'm done here, done with you.'

I see scuff marks on those wrists. I see uneven, broken nails. It's like she's falling apart.

She grabs the backpack, stands, turns, walks to the door.

I sit straight, breathe deeper, try to tell myself something smart but my attention is snared on this woman getting the hell out of my office. Silhouettes of strangers passing in the corridor now as she twists the handle. Above her head a carved wooden sign says, *'You are one decision from changing your life.'*

Dagny pulls the door open, not looking back.

And is that twenty million people I see walking away? Is that a whole heap of recognition, of some kind of stardom, some kind of fame I can monetize walking out my door?

I am of immense value and everyone can see it.

I breathe out, choose to rise above, say, 'Dagny...'

She turns, hand on the handle.

I go, '...sorry.'

Four

Assert: The greatest trick, if you can manage it, is to take absolutely nothing personally.

THAT big oak in the front garden is twice as high as the old stone house. There must be a hell of a view over the city from the top. Mim was up that thing so much, making videos and taking pictures with that mobile that I asked her one time. I said it would be good to see a pic or two. She took it badly and flew into an almighty rage. It ended with Fiz getting headbutted, attempted arson and us having to force-feed her a double dose of tranquillizers.

The thing with Mim was that if I'd told her she'd already agreed to take a picture up there, she'd probably have done it. If I'd said she had made a plan to make a video from the top of the tree, she'd likely have taken my word for it. We did learn paths through to her, little cheat codes like that which gave us ways to frame things, to progress with the days. But it was easy to make mistakes in the lightest conversations, to accidentally send her screaming from the house.

The phone had been useful, a way of keeping her busy while Fiz and I got on with things. It was never connected to Wi-Fi and didn't need to be. It was a distraction, a little games console, a calculator, a way for her to play preloaded tunes to herself. But it was also a means for her to see herself, to record some of what she was doing. We thought Mim witnessing Mim could become a powerful thing, something that could lead to some revelation, but that was just another stillborn hope. The plain truth was, as with managing some dismal habit, there was no solution. It was all just one day at a time.

There were pictures galore on the last day. Mostly close-ups of herself in the garden, in the tree, of her face smeared with mud. I saw her making videos of herself punching newly bloomed flowers into the ground, of her hurdling over hallucinated things that seemed to be dashing around. I remember watching on the CCTV camera at the front door that day as she tried to coax the farmer's big old tom down from our eight-foot fence. I knew well that the smart feline would not do as she wanted. It hadn't set foot on our grass since it watched her, stone in hand, crack open the skull of another moggie, perhaps its mother, brother, sister, a few months before. It may too have been uneasy after seeing our own cat, Frenchman, balled up, limbs quivering, in the centre of our sprawling ascending garden, mouth bloodied from ingesting a thousand fragments of a crushed light bulb. We never raised the issue of the unknown killed cat with the farmer, never did speak with him much in my time there. But I always felt he had some sense all was not well behind our high fences.

For part of the day, Our Trouble kept coming in and out, changing clothes over and over, sometimes with only a few minutes between. It was as if she was practising for some kind of transformation, some kind of drama. I got more and more uneasy about it all, sensing something truly treasonous had been making its way to the front of her mind. But, as usual, and usually for good reason, I said nothing to her mum.

Fiz wasn't coping. In those last days, she was mostly curled up on the sofa, white baseball cap pulled low, sometimes awake, sometimes less, often reading the horror stories of people who'd been in worse situations than us as a way to dilute her despair.

Fiz had hurt her hand, told me she might have broken a finger as she'd tried to disarm her daughter a few days before she died. Fiz said she had found her waving a stick around in the garden, thumping its end into the soft lawn. There was blood on her hand from where the skin was getting worn and broken with the force of it all. Fiz had approached and Mim had turned, whacked her hand and bent a finger in a direction it wasn't meant to go. To see my wife's hand bandaged, to see another big battalion of depression take her down a couple of hours later was too much, too sad, too hopeless.

In those last days, it was like we were waiting for something, like sitting among unexploded fireworks, certain that sooner or later something was going to blow. I'd thought again about finally reaching out, about pushing Fiz to at least have our case properly examined, but I hadn't had the heart to say it. It would, I know, have sunk her lower.

By 8PM, Mim was in pyjama bottoms and a woollen cardigan. She'd smeared gel into what was left of her yanked-out hair, her scalp half threadbare. She'd messed it up so madly that night to the point it seemed to mirror what was going on inside. She'd taken to walking, turning in small barefoot circles, stamping into the dirt, saying fast fluid things in what sounded like some eerie tribal rhythm. She talked and muttered and mumbled and occasionally broke off to throat out something louder, something primal. She came in and ran along the hall to her room a couple of times and, on one occasion, I heard her stop and my ears zoomed to the silence. I heard a scraping sound. But, given everything that day, in all those awful days, I let it go.

I turned to alcohol in an attempt to disconnect, to drink the ugly day pretty. There were moments when Fiz and I so badly needed priceless time away from the burned, scarred, semi-sighted dangerous catastrophe who shared our back-to-front home. I could tell on that night that Fiz too had noticed something more wayward about Mim, but she wouldn't say it. Maybe that's why we silently agreed to make the whiskeys a little larger, the mixers a little smaller.

Some of the rest is still a blur, and not just because of the drink. It's a blur too because I had this strong feeling that what was happening could not be happening. I've come to accept that this brain of mine battled from the start to hand me every detail, every frame of it all. I know the brain goes into a state of hyper-awareness at times of great intensity, great danger. It's as if it slows time, just as in a car crash. I know it's because it's deep processing the aggressive environment, analysing all the information it can, and it might save your life. Yet the effect is unreal.

A band was playing on the TV in the living room, some group promoting a tour. I'd been sitting on the sofa beside Fiz and stood up, heading for a pee. In the mirror, the big brass-framed rectangle above the fire, my eyes landed on Mim. She was at the front window and staring right at me, hair mad, unbidden rage all over her face, all fists clenched and spittle. It looked as if that face was crunching together as if the demons in her mind had forced her to suck it into the centre. She looked like a badly sewn scarecrow, like some kind of cartoon you'd keep from kids. It was obvious our

Did She See You?

resident lunatic, here staring from dark into light, needed a wide berth.

Her eyes, though degraded by sunshine, missile locked on me as I made my way across the room. I could see one of her hands was gripping hard on the neck of a bottle of cider, which wasn't good. We had learned, after she'd glugged down some wine passed to her by an alcoholic at a clinic, that booze amounted to an accelerant for Mim. Clearly, she'd got some more somewhere along the way, must have stashed it, ready to throw down her throat when those demons demanded. Liquor clashed with her meds and emboldened her plans and right then, I know... I know... I should've pulled it from her. I should've risked another punch, another kick, another fight as I once again tried to do the right thing. I'll openly admit in my book how I should've grabbed it and dosed her up with those brain-bombing pills. I should've risked another sleepless night with her camped at our bedroom door, of double-checking the lock every few minutes, of her growing stronger and screaming *'witches'* at us, of her trying to find a way to set herself or the house on fire. Instead, without a word to Fiz, I dropped the blinds.

I talked myself out of locking her outside as I went to the toilet. I passed new scrapes on the wall as I went along the hall, a metre long waist-height scrawl. I tried to read it but couldn't get the angle right and couldn't give a shit. I went to the bathroom, did my business, washed my hands, looked at my face, told me to stay calm, told me I was being tested, told me this was just a chapter in a story, that nothing lasts forever. I grabbed a novel, went back.

The front door was open. Mim was inside. I couldn't see where until I turned to the living room where I'd left Fiz. Our Trouble was just in the doorway, partly blocking me as I approached from behind. Her left arm, furthest from me, was lifted as if pointing. I looked to where it was directed, could see that Fiz was standing, that her eyes were still on the TV, that she was unaware of Mim at the doorway.

All in slow motion now, all in soft motion...
Fiz watching the screen. Mim watching Fiz.

I didn't speak, didn't want to speak, didn't want to engage Mim, hoped she'd just turn, that I could step out of her way, that she'd exit the house once again.

I could see Mim's short, thin, gaunt face in the fireplace mirror. I could see Fiz's head there too, her eyes pulling away from the TV, turning towards the door where we were. I could feel that Mim was bracing, tensing up as Fiz's head was turning from the screen. Mim's muscles were pulling together like she was about to jump. There was something black in her hand, the edge of something clean, angled, metallic. There usually was of course, but she held this thing differently. At first, I thought her arm was drifting, some indifferent sway away from her body, but I was wrong. The arm was locked on Fiz, tracking her mother's slow, blind approach. Fiz's eyes were turning more and would imminently reveal Mim just a few feet away.

And then I remember the hyper-awareness, the theatrical, the drama kicking in. The colours thickening, smudging, spreading across the room. Fiz's head, an inch more towards Mim, her eyes starting to take in the back of the room. And, soundless, a mark appearing on her temple like a fleck of black in a silent film. Fiz falling, dropping straight down, an instant vertical plunge out of sight as if her bones had turned to water.

Did She See You?

    Then some clapping on TV, people whistling their love for the band, for the song. Then the sharp, hard crack of the shot. It was like the sound had been seized, restrained and released only after the horror of the visible.

    And Mim was turning to me, arm still stretched, eyes vibrating in her head, face high-speed twitching, like all her blood and mud-smeared skin was alive with a billion parasites. That burned, scarred hand arcing around, that deadly crunch crashing on and on through the room.

    The sound stopped and I knew. Reality was arriving, although staggered and disjointed. I knew Fiz was dead. I knew a hole had been blasted into her head, that her funny, wild mind had been torn open and her life stolen as she stood in her living room. I knew Mim had just killed her mother.

    And in that long, wild, overloaded second a clear train of thought. Stripped of emotion, it said plainly that if one of those two lives was to be lost, I would not have wanted it to be Fiz. And I was immediately thinking that because of this deed, whatever love I had for Mim had been struck out. Our Trouble had become unwanted.

    I looked to see Mim aiming the pistol right at me, the barrel's exit hole clear. I didn't move, didn't speak. I looked away to where Fiz had stood, to the mirror that had pictured her alive one heaving moment before. My face in that mirror now, the side of Mim's head as she was about to kill again.

    Yet it was weird. Clear questions were bursting into life.

    What had been Fiz's last sight? Had she seen Mim as she turned? Did she know who killed her? Did she know she was murdered by the girl to whom she had surrendered her adult life?

    I looked back at the gun barrel and said, *'Did she see you?'*

Five

Assert: The obstacle becomes the way.

SHE used to say, *'You've got gold bones.'*
I'm standing in a supermarket and this comes into my head. In front of a large, refrigerated display of berries and nectarines and grapefruit and this happens. Such is the playful personality of grief. What was the trigger this time? The connection? What was the spark, the provenance? No idea. Right here, on this colour co-ordinated shop floor, in the absolute soul of indifference, I think about her saying *'gold bones.'*

But I don't mind this memory. It's inconvenient, disruptive, but it's one of the good ones. *Gold bones.* It has me smiling here, in front of the chopped pre-soup, here near the cheese. I stand still, chilling, serenaded by an old Bee Gees track, and embrace this uninvited gem.

'Gold bones,' I say.

Fiz would buy a carrot, check it for holes, check if anything was living inside. Things do live in carrots, she told me. She'd say *'due diligence'* as I watched her inspect, as I explained how she was a little weird about carrots. 'Some icky childhood cooking trauma,' she'd say. 'A slug had slid out during slicing,' she'd say.

She'd say, *'We are already in space'* anytime anyone mentioned space travel. We'd happily argue about it, me rooted to the ground, her twirling on a rock among the stars. She always had the better lines.

She'd say, *'Never apologise for correct actions'* and I feel all the time like I should be passing that on. I can't hear the word *'sorry'* without thinking of her, even though she never used it.

She'd say, *'If you're fearless you're immediately powerful'* and *'Snobbery is the worst vice'* and *'The bigger the front the bigger the back'* and *'Be brave enough to be hated.'* She'd say *'spare your emotions'* and *'patriotism is a weakness'* and *'adaptation is the story of the world'* and *'take nothing personally.'*

She'd say things and not pause, not leave a place for me to process, to react. She'd fill me up with little humming batteries of warm sentiment and energetic truth when every other insipid word in the day had left me running low. She'd say incisive things, leave this head crackling with excitement, get it bending itself around her phrases, admiring the speed of their construction, their strength once applied. She'd fill my heart with the future and ask about my day as this packed heart was taking off like an airship.

I'd say *'thanks'* to her sometimes, just for no reason, and she'd laugh and go, *'You've got gold bones.'* She'd say, *'Fluent in you, baby,'* and I'd say it back. She'd say, *'Hang for you, baby,'* and I'd say *'Hang for you.'*

Back then these bones felt shiny, clean, quality. Now they're tarnished, dirty, heavy. I feel like I'm stuck with them, that these gold bones sometimes pin me to the ground. They feel duller, colder, older, a burden.

I leave, drive to the little secluded beach at Quarrel Bay. It's a late afternoon that looks like an early morning now. The old spring day and new spring night are blending and soon the night will win. But in these minutes, it's easy on the eyes, clear, cool.

I strip at the back of the Land Rover, take off the big watch, throw it all in the boot, pull it closed. I walk

Did She See You?

over the spongy grass, over dead beings on the sand and enter the water, little wet thuds and splashes as I go. The timid animal brain voice says *too cold!* and I smother it, call on simple courage and relax and soldier on into the big water.

Into a thumping crawl on Belfast Lough, sawing out to the ferry lanes a mile away. It's a struggle but these shoulders are growing fast, my breathing more precise than ever, the mind now fused hard to commitment.

It's quiet out here when I stop. Little plops and drips, hard inhales and gasps as I tread, stay above the line. I'll write how when I come here it makes me think everything else stinks of dishonesty, that there's a truth to the smell out here. No masking scents of homes, shops, cars, planes, streets, people. There's a heavy, functional pong of diesel and fish here, the voluptuous utilitarian side-by-side. You hear everything here, feel everything, see far at every angle. Out here extends the senses, stretches the awareness. It's nature's free market. It slides in your mouth like a wet weapon out here where there's no safety net, no foothold, no lifeguard, no ladder to rest on and climb if you lose your step.

I'll write how I swim half as far as I can handle when I swim out and how it's an easy sum to get wrong. I'll write how with these gold bones I've felt the temptation to submit to the indifferent because it's exhausting all the time.

Fiz was right about it being liberating to know no one cares. She was right to say the number of people more than temporarily detained by anyone else's tragedy is less than their number of loved ones. She was right to say it's essential to understand that people don't care for your story, only for how it makes them feel.

    She'd said the big love lie gets told a billion times daily, that the little yellow smiley fib has become the currency of the world. She'd have understood why I go alone into these wet wilds because connection to everyone is disconnection, an eviction of involvement, a fracture of evolution. She'd understand that I'm staying here, marching alone in this honest, waxy grime, because knowing where the lies are is the greatest knowledge.

    She'd understand what I'm building here is the persistence to out-persist the biggest liar I know.

Six

Assert: Reputation is not built on intention.

I'LL talk about the big watch in my book. I'll be writing about the big Rolex and the story it tells. It's on when I'm working, off when I'm not. I'll say about the musky cologne too, the £200 a bottle stuff. And I'll write about the designer shirts and pants and socks and shoes.

I'll write how I imagine people saying, *'There's that guy with the bleached hair, the guy who drives the black Land Rover Discovery, the immigrant asshole who told a newspaper he's something called a mercenary life coach.'*

I'll write how they're saying, *'He used to be normal, that guy. Then his wife got shot and he started swimming in the buff every night. He cracked up, that guy. Turned into Mr Fake, that guy.'*

But most of the book will be about her, Our Trouble, all seventeen years of it. People are more interested in her than me. They're interested in how I coped, of course, but only because it's how I coped with the person who interests them most. They'll want to know how I feel about her, if I despise an unwell child, if an unwell child can truly earn an adult's hate. And I'll be totally honest about all of that. I'll be dangerously honest.

She's in front of me now saying, *'...were goose apparently in noma rit mate nps with new shades tucked into Lena's friend wave three times jesters of the old days and the laces...'*

Her small, pointed nose, her dead dry black hair, that thin, grated face, those fried, wet eyes.

'...*trying to get a work visa discovered the eggs locked last night don't chase the ace lol summits of India on one map easy feeling CMM85CT need to return an item Marco's skint legs refabricated dislocating nail facemask or we are through...*'

This is all we do, over and over again. A hundred or more times now I've sat here and let her mumbo jumbo her way through the hour. This is the very scene that stays the same, where two people meet and neither listens to the words of the other. Yet this scene right here will, sooner or later, be the point of change. My persistence will pay off. I am as certain of that as I am of anything.

I'll write how I imagine people tapping all this stuff into their phones. I'll say how I can see them poking those words she's saying into their laptops and tablets and pressing send, how I can see them dictating these messages to devices in their car or their kitchen. I'll write how I've entertained myself picturing the amazement on their faces as they learn a blurred eyed maniac who killed her mother has captured a copy of their little thought roll and revealed it to people in a nuthouse.

She'd take joy in knowing I've put flesh on some of her voices. But I will never let her know, never let her think for a second that I believe her horseshit. I won't give her that. As the one person on this ball of earth who knows her best and likes her least, I'll make it clear I knew from the start that although she's certainly ill, she's certainly lying about this anti-talent of hers. She does not believe what she claims any more than I do.

Did She See You?

A year or more before Fiz's death, Mim had a first go at explaining it all in her broken, stumbling, half-drunk, high eye-browed way of putting things. She'd said there were *'phone messages'* all around her and we said we knew, that everyone gets messages, that everyone's phone beeped and jingled and tooted and sang. So she'd thought hard and said, *'I see words coming out from where people are,'* and we'd smiled and told her this meant she was clever. She stood in front of us and rattled out a few random little phrases, word combos, and we said this was great and left it at that.

She said her head was feeling full, that stacks of these words were forming like long growths on the outside of her brain, all crammed together like shuddering towers of bricks and rocks. She said a shiny man was putting them there and pieces kept breaking away and spinning around and threatening to crash deep into her mind. Her only relief for her overloaded head, she'd said, was to let some of this stuff spill from her mouth, that she found tiny pieces of peace when she read from the piles of words clustering within, that it was a way of letting them go.

So because everyone just keeps being social with their media, because they keep messaging words and Facebooking words and Snapping words and Instagramming words through all of nature's space, more and more of them get received by Mim's invented supernatural antenna and stacked up inside her head.

The best of it, as one of the shrinks said to me, is that all of this makes her a sort of 'phenomenon'. Some experts reckon she's extraordinary because everything she says and does indicates that all of these words are imported, that they're not coming from within. They have no regularity or pattern, never appear to be a product of some other part of her mind. The shrinks are amazed by the way she never stops, that even when asleep this somehow inspirational unpoetry has been witnessed flowing out into this world.

I have to say that when the shrink said 'your daughter is a phenomenon, Mr Bic,' I clarified with her first that Mim is not my daughter before saying, 'It sounds like you believe her?'

And I think I then allowed myself a chuckle. I said to her, 'To be impressed by Mim's behaviour wouldn't you have to believe it was a genuine condition? Otherwise, she's just telling the longest lie on Earth and that cannot be impressive. Or can it?'

The shrink, Dr Harriet Hayward, told me, 'It is a real condition. That's not in doubt. It is real to her. One part of her mind is feeding another and to her it is as if another person or system is putting those words there, building them around her brain in myriad distinct constructions. What is fascinating, Mr Bic, is that she doesn't stop, that she keeps coming up with more and more random word strings which could be said to match random messages. That is what's phenomenal. From a psychological, medical point of view she's an exceptional case. In terms of the psychosis landscape, she's most certainly extraordinary.'

She said nothing about her murdering my wife, her own mother. She took no interest in Mim's being inspired more by damage than creation. She ignored how Mim was driven by hate and cruelty and the making of pain, that if there was any might in her character then it was there, in among the nasty, where it lay. The constancy of her output is no more than just voicing a voice we all hear in our heads all the time, I suggested. Where the rest of us are always thinking, she is always talking instead. It's just that what she thinks for the most part, for all of her infantile life, is nonsense. At its best, at its least damaging, it has been a long line of random, directionless crap, very often shouted at me or Fiz in the past, which has delivered neither her nor the world anything at all of use.

Yet with this spin of hers, she'd found a whole new way to trick. She'd managed to find a way to make the construction of phrasings in her head sound like random messages from outside her head. And the psychiatrists thought all this was great. This stuff, I told Dr Harriet, with all due respect, is not exactly rocket science.

Mim never did and does not have any thoughts of any weight. She fires out bits of thoughts, half considered sentiments, words stolen from films and songs, standard sign offs, numbers, celebrity names, over and over and over again. She parades a stream of garbage from modern life, just adds to the pollution of our times, in a very long and entirely one-sided conversation. To call Mim 'phenomenal' is to say the bottom of a paper shredder is phenomenal. To say she's phenomenal is to say you are impressed with a constant nothing.

What would be truly phenomenal would be for her to be telling the truth, for that brain of hers to have the power to mimic a digital receiver. Phenomenal indeed for her mind to be subscribed to a Wi-Fi service, to be so advanced it could instantly hack every dot and comma zooming through the air and have it come out of her mouth.

So let's put all that to one side. I'll be crystal clear when I tell anyone who reads my book that, with unassailable confidence, I can say Mim does not have such powers. Nor is she, I will assure them, in any way convinced she has such a power. She is, I will say, making the whole lot up on the spot. But they won't need me to tell them that, will they? I mean, when the details of her crazy behaviour go public, no one will believe them, will they?

'...get rice yoga yoga yoga harpooned in the straits while eyes open balls when praying Mount Pleasant Street you look amazing they were dancing in the sand dirty beast don't betting man G7 Mildred right mate your hole for single bitter pill...'

It was only a few hours after she killed Fiz that she went at it full time. As police started talking to her, she started pretending to tell them what was being sent through the air around her head. She conveniently started receiving and reporting messages non-stop on that day, just after she'd murdered her own mother. A coincidence? If you say so.

She's picking up your message to your friend, I'll write. I'll say how she's getting that text from your vets, that kiss to your lover, your hopeless WIN message to the talk show, your reminder from your dentist, the funeral itinerary for your old teacher, the location of your glasses.

A few months back I said to her, 'Hey Mim, why don't you get a job with MI5? You'd be invaluable.'

I said, 'Why don't you stand outside the White House and let the world know what's going on in there?'

I said once, over the din, 'You know I'll never believe you.'

I'll be making the point loud and clear that a lot of it is piss poor, no matter what the shrinks might think. It's not exactly a great feat of human ingenuity to say '... meet me at the café. Dave...' or '...leave the keys under the

Did She See You?

plant pot? Sara...' or *'...Lawrence. I will not buy the car due to behaviour at a horse race. Gavin...'*

I've said to her, 'Mim, no one believes you.' I've said, 'Miriam, you're making people hate you even more.'

I've said, 'Miriam, shut up, shut up, shut up – for Christ's sake, shut up.'

And she goes, *'...must end this Saturday last chance to catch one of the world's best-loved musicals scallions worship nothing routine Doctor Khan's early seen a million faces and Putin prefer toes with welcome joust bouncy pint harness in specks fifty odd dead on Australia fly time...'*

I'll be clear that I'm aware people are unsure about me too. I know I'll be saying all this about crackpot Mim and they'll be wondering about the quality of my thoughts, if maybe I'm lacking compassion. If they've seen any pictures of me since I set up in business, they'll have seen the garish Rolex, the crocodile here on my male breast. They'll have seen the little bits of show I wear, and I know that stuff makes people cynical. I've thought about how my look makes people think I'm just pretending to be a life coach, that I'm an act, a con man ripping off vulnerable cretins with sophistry while planning to dye my roots. Readers will be pondering benefits and doubts as I tell them how I have this thing about splashing on fancy smells every time I go to the door.

But I'll explain how there was a rebirth, how there's now a new version of me, that there had to be some new model because the old one was falling apart. I'll tell them there's a woman called Sue who carpet bombs my hair every 21 days. I'll say there's a mechanic called Karim who polishes up my Land Rover Disco every couple of months. I'll say my nails are manicured. I'll tell them I can't afford it at all, that I'm deep in debt but I'll say the point is I'm going somewhere, that all of it amounts to leaving whatever there was of the old me behind.

So go ahead, I'll say, and consider me some kind of physical lie, some kind of prancing dummy, some desperate peacock with gilded claws. Go ahead and judge me for what I say about a locked-up girl who thinks her brain is a phone. Hopefully, they'll come to understand how sometimes things change a person in unexpected ways and it doesn't matter what anyone else thinks. That'll be part of the point of the book.

I'm looking at her now, at the slight, dry, scarred, burned, odd skinny slip of humanity and I try not to be sad in the same way I try not to be angry. One day it'll all change, this stalemate we share. One day the word binge stops. One day she'll reframe, reboot, look up and we'll take the first step in a new direction as we all must do after destruction.

Patience is power.

And any day now.

Any day. It could happen on any one of these visits.

I wish it could be today.

It's still possible.

Come on, Mim.

Look at me.

Right now.

Today.

Make it today.

'*...regimental precursors were outlined in the first series get dead moving the barrel is hardly within bring the balance gypsy sitting looking pretty don't put the*

Did She See You?

fertile come home now love Stephen half five probably hotter than used to if it was forward it needs repainted your turd in my bog damn it's peas thanks for your entry broken you owe me...'

Something about going to Rome, something about a gastric problem, something about a dog, an orgy, a shoe, a plate, a parked-up Renault, a flag, some wires. Something about a password, crisps, a new desk, a hand job, a holdall. The meaningful rendered meaningless. Spam, spam, spam, spam, spam, a burst piñata of bullshit.

I say, 'Did she see you?'

'...could shite a better smoke standing among thorns with celebrated ingredient of them all give over and redeem them ffs allez vous en chief executive to hand back XX let them know if Dam Square version arse is humming wrought...'

'Did she see you?'

'...Huxley's torment bald wig bringing bricks to the second one a cut price involvement with alleged pirates and Julia's skills could collect Ballyvalhalla end of history the best of them relegated for me love mum be the greatest day obviously Italian banshee don't trample on masons steely knife third door on left Don...'

'Did she see you?'

'...buys Investment Weekly as part of expansion subscribe to pewdiepie write with fists put the string into the loop trouble in America reputations are not built before catching Sunderland if you don't have time to visit the pepperoni nips club...'

'Did she see you?'

Jason Johnson

Seven

Assert: Don't absorb, observe.

IN one of the boxes on my screen there's a woman who calls herself *GoodShotForABlindGirl.* There are twenty or so life coaches in little boxes as part of this local Zoom conference and everyone is using their name but her.
What does she mean?
This has been going on for more than ninety minutes now. Some people look like they're falling asleep but the host is still talking. Most of them would just go ahead and close their eyes if they weren't so used to pretending to strangers they give a hoot. We are a screen of coaches listening to stories about other coaches. I've seen so many smiles come and go, so much head cocking and mirroring and active eyebrows. It's all fake, all part of the tricks and lies, the mirrors upon mirrors.
I've said nothing. I should've chipped in when prompted like some of them did. I should've been more generous with my misery, my broken heart. I should've said she was shot in the head and that grief morphed into enthusiasm, that loss turned to gain and that I do what I do today in her name. I just sat in my box instead. But I know they all know my story.
Right now, I am the highest value alpha male in this Zoom call.
Short blonde hair, sipping an energy drink. Stocky, sturdy. Looks like she enjoys high tar and low lights, like a strong swimmer who chooses to go no further than the off licence. Her shirt looks like

Did She See You?

something a pilot would wear, black stripes down the light blue arms. She's hoping it makes some kind of point about who she is. Everyone here is trying to make some kind of point about who they are. Except she's the only one with a name that isn't a name.

GoodShotForABlindGirl

She takes another slug from that energy drink. One of those long, thin, creepy cans. I can't make it out but I bet it's called FIGHT or DYNAMO or KILLA or something. WHACK or THRUST or BELTER or something.

She coughs now, puts the can down. It's like she heard me thinking. I'm looking right at her and thinking energy drinks are the soft drink choice of the unhinged. I'm thinking how she's around my age, too old to drink that shit with any dignity and that I like the way she's been doing it all the same. I'm thinking she maybe knows herself, how that's the greatest thing. That slop will be called something like CHARGER or CRUSH. It'll be all CAF-ME-HARD and YO and RENDERBUK.

I am a high value alpha male and I am loaded with badass confidence right now and I believe nothing else.

'Hi Denis,' she says. 'I'm Bet.'

Holy shit. A private message.

I freeze, pretend my camera feed has stalled. I don't know what else to do. I don't blink.

'Hi?'

Shit. How long can I do this for? Or should I just exit?

Shit.

No. I have to move.

High value.

'Hi back,' I say.

I could ask if that hard caffeine she's drinking is called ROCKFIRE? I could tell Bet I bet it's called BUSTER, or maybe IMPACTER or the BANG BANG CAN, the BEAST, the FIREFORCE, the CRACK, the MIGHT, the HOWL.

But what about that name? The on-screen one. *GoodShotForABlindGirl.*

What does she mean? Is that about Mim? Is Bet about to ask about death? Does she want to know what it's like to see your spouse get shot in the head? Is she going to ask if I ever see my wayward stepdaughter, if I coach her when I visit her in that feared mental facility where monsters dwell?

She goes, 'Enjoying the conference?'

I read it and read it again. I'm not and should say so.

The host is talking about a paranoid client and it's like he's talking about me. He's asking if anyone has workable strategies for such a problem and people are all staring and I have no idea what I'm doing here.

Is Bet approaching me because my wife died? It's not like the whole country doesn't know the story. Everyone here, at this salt lick for small traders of the well-placed assertion, knows my story. What am I doing here? I can't be in the right place when I'm just sitting here thinking about simultaneously vacuous and foggy all this stuff is. All this is the nebulous business of inspiration and momentum, of bottling and teaching a side effect of reality. We sell ourselves with a riddle in which what cannot be done gets done. I've been telling clients the *impossible* can be done and I can't stop thinking that I'm purposely confusing *impossible* with *hard-to-do*. What if one was to say, 'But if it's *impossible* then how...?'

Did She See You?

I tell them to tell themselves, 'I'm a finisher.'
I tell them to tell themselves, 'A fighter fights.'
I tell them to say, 'No one does what I do,' to say, 'This is my time,' and 'Someday isn't a day,' and 'The only verb you need is to conquer.'

I have all these things ready to dispatch on-demand. I've learned a thousand of them, text a fresh one to my phone every morning, read it every hour, repeat it over and over. I spout these little boosters and gems off-the-cuff to clients like I know what I'm talking about. Yet sometimes I see the right words land at the right time and they think 'holy shit, that is amazing,' and everything makes sense for a moment.

I tell them to listen carefully to what I say because I know it's true, that it takes just one decision to turn your whole life around. I tell them I know it can be done because I've done it. This stuff, I say, has moved me up from rock bottom. It's what saved me, I say, from a watery grave. And they love that, love a comeback, love a triumph right in front of them.

Bet is smiling. I smile back. Who knows if she's looking at me?

Some guy has chipped in to say he's a fan of some Californian coach called HWKC Roundly and everyone nods as if they've heard of him. Some guy is saying HWKC Roundly says to flip stuff, flip everything, flip the real estate in your head, flip is the future. He says Roundly advises that if people reverse the pattern a new one will emerge.

Some guy says he takes that on board when he tells paranoid clients that they're probably right to be paranoid. And that sounds like terrible advice, anti-advice.

Some guys says, 'I'd say to a paranoid client, "*You're probably right to be paranoid about it. And when I say probably, I don't mean probably as in there's a chance you're right about this. I mean probably as in there's about an 80 per cent or a 90 per cent chance you're right. They ARE talking about you. They ARE laughing and mocking. Non-stop. I mean, who could pick up on this more accurately than you? Who could know better than you?*"'

Bet must know Mim's half-blind. So why would she use that name? *GoodShotForABlindGirl?* Does she know I cradled my wife's broken head as Mim climbed a tree and aimed a pistol at arriving police and was almost blasted out of the branches by a marksman as a helicopter chopped overhead? Why would she have that name if she knew that? What does she mean?

Some guy is saying, 'I'd tell her "*Knowing they are talking about you means you are alert, wide awake, tuned to your environment, owning and applying the knowledge you need. And application is where the changes get made, isn't that right? So your next step is to work out how you're going to first defend yourself in the short term, then how to extract yourself from this most awful and unwarranted attack on your character. I mean, it's ruining your life, all this non-stop talking about you, so you need to develop an escape plan. Don't you? Or it could kill you. Couldn't it?*"'

Bet's staring either at me or at this maniac doing the talking. She folds her arms and I'm wondering if it is because she's pissed off or defensive or bored. I bet Bet wants to grab that VALIANCE or DEMONBLOOD right now, wants to stick a long vodka in it, tip it to her face and pour.

Did She See You?

And some guy says, 'And then I'd say *"You might be right but there's a small chance you might be wrong too. If you're right, you need a different life. You might need to cut ties, move away, leave the country. You certainly need to quit your job right away. That's a no brainer. So you've plenty of planning to do to get this right.*

"But if they're not talking about you all the time, then that's where I can help. That ten or maybe twenty percent chance you're wrong? That's what I can answer, that's what I can conquer, where I can deliver you good things. You have a decision to make. If you want to hear about the twenty percent, then great.

"But, if not, you need to wrap this up right now. I'll give you your money back and you can quit your job, leave town and start again.

"Or if you want to hear me out about the twenty per cent? If you want to hear about the one chance in five that you're wrong? You can stay and hear it."'

Some guy goes, 'That's the way into the client's thinking. Move that person onto your ground but let her think she's going there voluntarily. And get it out early in the hour, leave plenty of time so that walking out of your office seems pointless.'

And all the people in the boxes are nodding and some are holding up hands and doing a little fake applause. Bet's still staring at me and I can't look at her anymore. I haven't even replied to her question about enjoying the conference.

I write, 'No. Why are you called *GoodShotForABlindGirl?*'

She pushes her lips together, narrows her eyes and writes, 'I'm not.'

And I look at her name and she's not.

Eight

Assert: If you meet no enemies, you are going the wrong way.

A PHONE placed between my Americano and blueberry muffin. I look up and there's two of myself in enormous mirror sunglasses. I appear disappointed. I look back at the phone. A locked, blank, black screen. A little, wide and crooked finger pushes it closer. She takes the seat opposite.
'What is this?' I say.
'It's a phone,' she says. 'Notice it's not recording. Just so you know.'
I am high value and calm as a cool wind.
'Okay,' I say. 'You're making a point of some kind, Ms O'Reilly?'
'Yes,' she says. 'That I have no interest in you.'
'Good. I thought you'd be back in California by now.'
She's taking off a flowery face covering, goes, 'What kind of screensaver do you use?'
'What?'
'What's your screensaver? On your phone?'
'None of your business.'
'Is it your late wife?'
'None of your business.'
I am a high value alpha male and I'm proving it with my words and actions.
'Well okay,' she says, 'not my business.'
'I have a lot of questions at this very moment.'
'No shit,' she goes, taking off her little backpack, her black jacket, sitting down, 'me too. I've been

Did She See You?

thinking a lot. The first question is, like, are you going to stay in this rocky puddle of a city all your damn life? I mean, you're not from here, right? So what's holding you here? I guess you can't turn your back on Miriam, right?'

And she's reaching into the backpack, rummaging around, her head tilted forward as if it's interesting in there. It's blue now, her hair. It's sky blue with unabsorbed fresh raindrops trickling down. It's awful, like some piercing scream for attention. Her white tee-shirt has two black dots where her nipples would be, a red smile at the diaphragm. She looks more square than blobby today, an emoticon whose been working out. I'm thinking that terrible style is her style.

She looks up, pleased, and puts a leather glasses case on the table.

'For you,' she says.

I clear my throat to speak. The only thing that comes to mind is harsh and I park it. I open the case and can feel the luxury as I do. Inside, sunglasses just like the ones she's wearing.

'A gift,' she says, 'to make your world darker so you feel more comfortable in conversation.'

Still holding the box, I say, 'Why are you here?'

'You could put them on at least say "Cool, thanks Ms O'Reilly."'

I lift them out, slide them on. Ray Bans. Aviators. Mirrors. No idea what they might cost. I like them. In this crowded coffee shop under a cloudy Irish sky, everything looks better.

'Cool. Thanks, Ms O'Reilly,' I say.

'No problem. Call me Dagny.'

'Why are you here?'

'In here? It started raining and I don't like that kinda thing. You like rain?'

'Why are you still in Belfast?'

'Ah, gotcha. My flight's not for a few days. Lots to do before then, as I said. You like to think I ran away all wounded and homesick because you kicked me out of your pit of an office, don't you?'

I say, 'Is this just coincidence? You being in this café at the same time as me?'

'Café? This is Starbucks, man. You don't say café for Starbucks.'

'Okay, Starbucks. Is it a coincidence?'

'Sure it is. Small town. I've been travelling around, just got off the bus, was walking along, it started raining. Didn't even see you until I walked inside. You know that kind of thing happens in the real world, right?'

'So how come...'

She knows the next question, knows the answer. She turns a meaty hand around, points a sausage back over a shoulder. Sunglasses shop right across the street.

'I see,' I say. 'Expensive impulse buy.'

She goes, 'Yeah whatever. I'm very rich.'

'Okay,' I say. 'Because of your twenty million non-friends.'

'I'm aiming for twenty-two million non-friends by year's end. Almost twenty-one now. They're really digging the interviews. And they'll love the stuff I'm getting here, in this town. My subscribers are totally plugged-in and interested people. But a lot of it's in the editing, y'know?'

'So what stuff are you getting here?'

'Jeez man, you have no clue what's going on. You still haven't checked my channel?'

'As I said, no interest.'
'You should.'
I go, 'I'm 39, Dagny. I'm a little old for your channel. I don't want to know about it, to see it or to be interviewed on it.'
'Hey, thanks. And did you notice I didn't ask you?'
'Whatever.'
'Truth is though, Denis - can I call you Denis? The truth is you'd be perfect for that interview. I'm no longer interested and would say no even if you asked now, but you'd be perfect. You're a peacock. But I don't want you anymore, so there's that.'
'A peacock?'
'Sure. Blonde hair, weird clothes. All knock-offs. I mean WTF right? Those little big shoulders. All that supercharged scrawny, right? You must be working out a lot, man. Maybe it cheers you up. And the story. Sheesh! The crazy daughter locked up on the hill with her kooky folks goes ahead and murders her mother because of some reason or other that isn't clear. Isn't that right?'
'No. Anyway, thank you for your sympathy.'
'I won't insult you with sympathy. You have my empathy. But you know that. You get me, Denis. You get me.'
'I don't.'
'You see, I want to disrupt. I need to. It's the way forward. The hard path is usually the right one, don't you think?'
'It's your life.'
'You have no clue about my generation, Denis. We are open-minded and understanding. We're the guys who can change our gender or get paid for playing games or showing ass in our rooms, you know? We're

all in loving communities, all supported and supportive, reaching out to everyone. In all of human history, Denis, we might be the easiest, nicest, most compassionate people yet. Secrets are dead, man. Privacy is dead and it doesn't matter. Get over it. That's the difference between us, Denis. You just can't feel alive among your fellow humans, you can't share. You just scuttle off into the darkness. Life coach, my ass. You should handle your own problems first, man.'

It's important to take nothing personally when a high value alpha male.

I go, 'Your generation likes you because you sit around telling them how great they are for doing nothing else other than watch you.'

She goes, 'Of course,' as if there's nothing worth considering in what I just said.

She's looking at the muffin now, not sure why. I'm waiting for a fat little hand to pull a piece off. I see a fresh mark on her face, a bruise emerging on the left side above the eye, starting on the forehead and dropping below. And there's more damage behind those mirror shades, I reckon.

'What happened?' I ask, pointing, my finger aiming at her twice, my face watching it happen infinite times. 'Your head, your eye. Is someone harassing you here?'

She smiles and the total symmetry is even more total with my two mirrored faces in her face. She ignores my question, smacks her lips to dismiss it.

'It's kinda cool for me being here,' she says, 'feels like the right place to be. You know at home I have an Irish wolfhound? I know they're not like an Irish thing, like wolfhounds aren't running around the streets here or anything, not like sacred cows or anything. But it's an

Did She See You?

Irish thing, right? Does that make sense? I miss my big guy. My girlfriend is keeping him for me while I'm away, but I know he's missing me. Dogs are great. I give a lot of money to dog shelters in California and I'm known for it.'

I do a half-smile. 'Look, Dagny, I don't want to be...'

'You'll notice,' she says, pointing at the phone in front of me, 'I'm not checking that while in your company. That's not easy for me. I'm like a digital addict. That's a real thing, you know. But I'm controlling it, standing strong. It's hard, I guess, but I'm doing it out of respect for you, peacock.'

'You'll notice,' I say, 'that I came here for a quiet cup of coffee.'

She doesn't have one, I'm thinking. She's maybe waiting for me to ask for her order, to queue and get it. That would be the decent thing to do but I know she'd take it as a signal to hang around annoyingly, like an unread text, for as long as she could.

She goes, 'So, Dense, how many clients have you got?'

'What?'

'How many clients have you got?'

'You just called me Dense?'

And she genuinely stops moving, freeze frame. She turns her face slightly to one side as if directing an ear my way.

She says, 'Come again?'

I go, 'Did you just... what did you call me?'

She straightens again, goes, 'Your name. I called you Denis.'

'Okay.'

'So, like, is it okay if I call you Denis?'

'Yes. That's okay.'

74

Maybe it's the background noise here. Maybe I'm doing some paranoid thing, some arrogance thing. Not enough sleep, maybe. Bad diet, possibly. I'm still working on myself. I steal a glance at the silent young man and woman at the table beside us. They're both on their phones and I wonder if they're listening, if they heard me being called Dense or if they're too absorbed in their screens to hear. They both look at me at the same time and smile.

Dagny goes, 'Hey. So I asked how many clients you have? And PS, I don't use the word Dense. Maybe if I was talking about physics or some shit, but not to refer to people.'

'What?'

'How many clients?'

'Yes,' I say, 'clients?'

She goes, 'Yeh.'

'What difference does that make to anything?'

She goes, 'Three questions in response to my one question. So I'm guessing you have...'

'What do you care?'

'I'm guessing you have... three. Five tops. Am I right?'

'Whatever you think.'

'Okay. Six. Tops. Not exactly Tony Robbins, right?'

'Whatever. We have no business to discuss and that sounds like business.'

'So, you haven't even looked me up yet? Googled little Dagny O'Reilly, California's cutest fatberg?'

'No.'

'Seriously?'

'Seriously.'

'Sheesh.'

'Right.'

Did She See You?

'Do you know eighteen percent of my subscribers very regularly buy merch?'

'I didn't know that, no.'

'These people are active, energetic, eyes wide open, constantly communicating, recommending and always looking for direction. That's value right there, in the commercial sense, in the whole human sense too. I like to think I make the two overlap.'

'Right.'

'I can think of like zero companies and like zero people who wouldn't want to be a guest on my channel.'

'I can think of one.'

'Well, I can...'

'Dagny – go away.'

'Ah, peacock...'

And it's annoying me, that peacock thing. It's annoying me that she's come to tell me all about herself again and I need to end this now.

I look her in the eye, mirror to mirror, go, 'Get away from me, okay? I don't want to talk to you. I don't want to know you. I don't want your sunglasses.' I pull them off, send them spinning across the table. I go, 'You must understand I don't like the reason why you and your wolfhound and merch are interested in me in the first place. Your interest is painful to me, Dagny. I want you to stop.'

She looks down, back up at me. She's embarrassed. She's got nothing.

'We're done here,' I say, firm whisper. 'And, you know, I can't believe it's the second time I've had to say this. This stuff of mine, my life, my loss – it's not some fodder for your bullshit subscribers, your bullshit angst-ridden fat kids and dopamine-hooked gender-fluid shooting masturbators and cyberbullies, right? I'm asking it now, most clearly - get out of my life.'

She reaches for the jacket, the backpack, the phone, says, 'Hey, slow the roll, man. I was saying hello. I've said already I don't want you for my show anymore anyways. And you're a rude asshole, you know that?'

'Yes,' I say, 'Sometimes I have to be.'

Her face says she's got it. The lips purse. She stands, pulls the coat on, slides on the pack, turns, walks, a whisper in the air as she goes, something about mirrors. Maybe *other people are your mirrors.* Maybe something like that.

I turn, watch her go, see the nosy screen addicts at the table beside leaving too, giving me the evil eye as they do, offended by none-of-their-business. They're just like Dagny and she's just like them, like everyone else living the screen life, every other outsourced personality, every other human exclamation mark in a vast electronic sewer where nothing ever exits, nothing degrades, nothing gets flushed away and it all just circulates forever.

I look back at the muffin, still untouched. At the sunglasses case, the mirrored glasses still there, showing me to me. I take a sip of coffee, take out my phone, look back again to see if I can see her but she's gone.

I dictate, 'Anxiety instructs that you are likely to fail. Confidence advises that it doesn't matter if you do. Which one is more likely to lead to success? This thing we call confidence can have more value than gold, than oil. Someone like me can teach ways to mine it, to bring it to the surface. And how to begin? It's simple. You must lie to yourself, you must tell yourself that, from this moment, confidence is spilling into your blood, that it is coursing through every muscle, that it is rushing around every part of you as we speak.'

I save it. There's the kernel of an idea in there. Needs work, but there's something in there I can develop.

I look at the Rolex, the Submariner model I take off before I swim, the one that flew here from China wrapped in news pages I couldn't read. I'm thinking about confidence now, thinking about all the books which say 'fake it until you make it' as the Asian hand sweeps its timeless lie around the copied Swiss face.

And I picture my blue Lacoste polo shirts, black and maroon. I picture their fading crocs and washed-out labels, their uneven seams loosening from waist to neck.

I'm thinking about my dying Land Rover, that ailing Disco, revamped over and over, fitted with parts from workshops with no listed address.

And I feel him coming now, striding towards me from among the crowds on the street outside. I push the coffee and food away in familiar readiness as I sense his stamping proudly through the door, the long black sheet dragged behind. I feel it as grief struts high-kneed past the tables in here, whipping up a mean, sharp wind as he goes. I feel his stare on my back and know that no one can see him, that he's not there and I'm too frightened to look. My muscles fail as the rhythm of his footfall powers me down. He's grief today or guilt today or both of those things and I don't know what he knows and I don't know what he wants but when he shows he wins. He's too bold to confront, too qualified to duel. He's perfectly engaged, brilliantly matched with his job, a man who drags that thick black sheet behind to pull right over my head as he passes. He comes to cover me, to stop and wait while the cape of ink falls and blinds and beds down into all the corners and curves of my head, face, body. He'll circle me in my darkness and whisper the tiniest details of what she's like as she lies there, a hole in her head, all her curated wonder spilt.

    My head is tipping now for his arrival, his instant night around me, my face falling onto the hard sunglasses, onto the cold table, publicly falling apart.

Nine

Assert: Simplicity is the ultimate elegance.

    ID check. Sniff from a dog. No food, no drugs. A look in the eye, nod of a head. They know me well by now. Through a door frame with no door. A beep, another nod. No leg spread required. They know the watch as I remove it, leave it in my tray. They know the hair as a man looks me up and down. They know the situation as I smile, remove the belt, step away.
    The smell starts here, as you go from entering to entered. The smell of what lives here, the long smell of trauma. It's territorial, advisory, instructive. It decants as you move around, breathes itself onto your clothes, your skin, tries hard to stay with you when you leave, dies hard in the nose. A smell of bygone abuse, of new violence, of piss and cabbage, of longed-for needs, of pointed wrongs, of immovable brokenness and rushing anger. It's the smell humanity makes when it goes bad from the inside, when it crashes out in all sorts of quaint or interesting or catastrophic ways.
    They say don't worry about the scent, don't let it dig into you. They say most of it's in your mind, that you're exaggerating the rest. This place is aired, clean and organised, they say. It's as safe and sound as anywhere could be in this world, the newest and best place of its kind. They say your senses are just getting ahead of themselves, and all you're smelling is a community with different patterns, on different chemicals, a regularised largely indoor society that isn't the one you know. Right here is New Ready House, a cutting-edge new village for the criminally insane, a

state-of-the-art facility for the ones who smashed, maimed and killed as they put themselves at the centre of their own horror stories. This is where the monsters are.

'Mr Bic.'

'Harriet. You can still call me Denis.'

It's always mister at first. She does it on purpose, a professional habit to disdain the social, to keep the line drawn in a business where lines of all kinds are important. Mr Bic helps keep walls high and circle small.

We walk as she tries to sum up the latest news.

Harriet's never late, never leaves me hanging, never annoyed, never too busy. She thinks with her face, is as honest as a human can be and never wants to say the wrong thing. I've a theory that her smartness is immense, her kindness unrequited. She's tall, longer than her short, simple devout-looking face suggests. And she's got these little legs, this stretched back, this low centre of gravity which gives her an elegant trunk and a furious walk. She'd be a great midfielder, but I wouldn't say it.

She goes, 'Nothing of note to report. Quieter from around twenty-one hundred as normal, unclear whispering during sleep, begins turning the volume up on waking at oh six hundred, but not now to the point she's annoying others. In a way, you could say she's become more considerate, which is progress given her conditions. But look, I'll catch up with you after you've met, okay?'

'Sounds good. Thanks.'

The briefings before the meeting are a courtesy. They don't like to say much without the client there. They like to discuss the issues in front of the issue, in

Did She See You?

front of the issue's visitor. It's some kind of Glasnost strategy in this radically experimental hub which, some report somewhere says, helps the mad stop thinking they're guilty. The criminal isn't criminal here. Crime doesn't exist here. Inmates go from criminal to sectioned to patient to guest. Reality is switched off and I can hear it in the unchallenged declarations from residents, the energetic yells turning ordinary words into frightening imagined images.

Harriet stops, turns, swipes a card. A comforting warm, green minty glow blossoms around a white door's silver handle. It unlocks with the noise of a chocolate bar snapping.

She reaches up, straightens glasses that are way too big for her face. I have a feeling they're not real.

I watch the door opening itself so precisely, so slowly, with perfect electronic grace.

I go, 'Thanks.'

She smiles, half her face shooting up for half a second as if to say 'it's nothing.' She scuttles gracefully off to do what it is she does. I go through the lovely, impenetrable door and it closes beautifully behind me as the green glow fades.

I can walk down at least some of this corridor unescorted these days. I'm trusted here, part of the scenery now, just another guy who found his place among the crazy. I don't complain about anything. I'm one of the few who doesn't. I don't insist on progress for Mim, don't ask what treatment she's getting, what she eats, reads, watches. I don't ask what she wears, how often she gets outside, who she likes, who she hates, who she tries to hurt. They think I'm easy going about all of that stuff because I trust them to do the right thing. The truth is I've found no way to ask because I've found no way to accurately explain how I feel about her, no way to explain how I care about her care.

Tables attached to the floor. Lightweight vases. Small, bright rugs. Orderlies milling around, pastel shirts, smiles and nods. Patients in T-shirts chatting with each other. This could be anywhere at first sight. Could be an all-inclusive destination, the social point of a college, the inside of a high-tech firm. Weightless plant pots and calm paperbacks on shelves, a yoga class, chess and cards, tablets in foamy skins. There's a little climbing wall, a gym, an art studio, a kitchen, bean bags, a movie, a dance class. The pictures on the walls are by clients, selected by staff. They're what you'd see anywhere, but take on a whole new richness in this place. They're pictures that chime with the smell, the shouts.

That blurry pencil sketch of the shaggy-haired mother with the infant was drawn by Martin – who set fire to his girlfriend's home and killed her on the street outside with a brick because she called him racist.

The blue dashes for sky, the yellow dashes for earth, the perfect red crayon square in the middle, the work of Sophie – she cut a man's cock off and slit his throat in the toilet of the 9AM from Belfast to Bangor because she thought he was 'from the bible'.

The fifteen smiling, pink faces in among a dozen green trees are courtesy of Marco who was ordered by a demon to hammer his sister's baby's feet to a pulp before throwing the child and his sibling out of the window of the hotel room in which he claimed to have lived for two hundred years.

That wispy, fading figure, all chequered yellow and black, holding both its hands up, the palms open, the hands swapped, the thumbs on the outside –

straight from the felt tips of Miriam, who shot her own mother with a stolen pistol and has social media running through her head.

That drawing, to my knowledge, is the total of her creativity here. Drugged to the eyeballs, she muttered about salt and blackbirds and garden sheds during her first week at New Ready, took to holding the pens and making her mark on that one sheet of A3. Dr Harriet did well to get that much out of her before Mim got the better of whatever compliance chemicals they'd issued. She gave up on art to instead focus exclusively on her lie.

I reach the visitors' centre door, another thick white pretty slab fit to stop another tank and as usual, this one's already open. The green, radiant flush around the handle, the invisible concierge welcoming one and all.

The smoothness of everything in here, the gear change inescapable after entering from the rainy day outside, from the packed car park under that platoon of black cameras.

The Kenyan orderly is recent. He sits at a desk to the left, cardboard cups of water and a plate of biscuits at his side. He smiles me in, nods his head towards Mim in the back corner beside the big round window. I look over and see that the rain has stopped, see the bright plants growing in sunlight around her. Her face is tipped forward, untended patches of hair just long enough for her to tuck behind ears, one or other hand rising every few seconds to ensure not a strand has strayed. The weak, straight shoulders at perfect right angles to her neck reveal she's jabbering away, pretending she's under constant siege from the modern world, a victimised human mailbox trying to convince us all the fake is real and real is fake.

Six other clients here, all meeting friends, relatives. Most of them are doped hard, trippy, docile, sort of happy, sort of responsive. There's no cocktail they can't design, no attitude they can't engineer, no mood that can't become something else in here with the right recipe. I told them once how I felt Mim was sleepy, dozy, unawake, that she was even more unavailable than usual, as if she was on slow. It was just an observation, one offered when prompted, a few unconsidered words. And on the next visit she was on fast forward, a livewire upgraded to my specifications. I've barely said a thing to them about her since.

I look at her now, hived off, separated, outcast among outcasts, sectioned off from the sectioned because of her babbling, her endless, useless, massive monologue. It's the constancy of it all, more so than the tiny volume, which over time could drive even the mad mad.

I watch from this end of the room as a hand goes up, as nervous fingers flash and tuck hair. I get angry, briefly, look away, reframe. It's common, that kind of stuff. It's normal. It's even expected. Little waves of it come and go in here. And here it is again. Right now, looking back over, I'm pissed off.

I check first with the orderly.

'Anything interesting?'

He stands, goes softly, 'I don't think so. Things are the same.'

I go, 'Thought so. It's Shab? Is that right?'

'Shadi.'

'Ah yes. I apologise.'

'No problem, Mr Bic. My name is short for Shadrack.'

'Shadrack from the bible?'

'So they say,' he says, mellifluous east African tones.

I go, 'I won't forget again, Shadi.'

He shrugs and we both smile as if there's something to smile about.

It really is calming in here. There's lots of even light on the clean walls, lots of interesting shapes and curves and bends to the room. It makes for the perfect drug den.

I walk through visitors and visited towards Mim. I drop down opposite into the soft yellow desk chair and exhale. Our little face off once again. Our little game once more. I don't even say 'hello.' I don't give her that because there's no point. Our Trouble has never said 'hello' to anyone in her life.

The words are running smoothly, easily, a quick and even tempo, a ticker tape of lies. There's a pipe being bought, a notice of approval, a line of curses, a jogger sweating, a fact, a joke, a pregnancy, a meeting, a horse through a fence. A hand tucks hair. Her little ears are ornate in their detail yet pointless on that head.

I listen more and know I could switch it off if I wanted, stop hearing it if I chose. It would be as normal as not hearing my own heart, not seeing my own nose. But, on arrival, I need to listen, to check, to survey, to calibrate. I need to read her as best I can. She's tick-tocking gently, barely tilting from side to side, fingers lightly fidgeting, living her deception with perfect economy.

'...bus passed with driver rubbing his eye no more than £4k tweet your arse Plan A takes from Plan B life is decay in a big country assigned at birth why...'

There was a power cut in the winter. The lights gave and for a second we were in something close to dark. I saw her look up when she wasn't sure if I could see her clearly. For a second, just one second, she stopped talking. It wouldn't have been noticeable to anyone else, but for me it was like a shaft of light, a burst of grace. The lights kicked back in and she went to nowhere normal again, back to that verbal hyperinflation, head forward once more, the long lie unspooling, unwinding and running out some more.

'Did she see you?'

'...the same bin...'

'Did she see you?'

'...depuis vendredi dare Plan C ffs...'

'Did she see you?'

'...clunk before you drag leaves you can't waste promise...'

'Did she see you?'

Who knows what she could see that time, in the dark, when she looked up. Her vision is very much reduced now from what it was, sclera all creamy white, all tanned by the sun. Yet who knows what colours are clear or not to her because the feedback is so poor.

'...the back of my balls was in the same congratulations Mersey...'

'Did she see you?'

'...my charger mate dictionary is hate speech dogger who got my money...'

Who knows where they begin and end, all these little somethings she makes into nothings.

'... people I can no longer bear dropdown menu confidence tramps like us...'
'Did she see you?'
'...salads are number plate...'
I know she always knows I'm here. I know she knows what I'm asking. I know she has an answer and I know she knows I know. It took me a few weeks, but I came to know that she talks faster in the moments when I ask my question.

There was never any sign of her showing any understanding of what she'd done, of her recognising the death of her mother, of how she came close to killing me, to killing cops who stood under that tree. There was only silence until the words began at the police station, after they got her to drop the gun, after they climbed up, met her halfway. The words have been running since that night, all through the assessments, all through the stimulation and over-stimulation and de-stimulation. What she had been toying with in the months before the murder became a full-time mission.

At first the police and every other professional thought she had something to say, something to explain, a secret to tell. There was an urgency about it, a drama in the way she spent herself in those first days which fascinated them.

But soon enough they realised she was just saying what gets said by everyone else all the time. They worked out, with assistance from myself, that she was just saying anything she could think of. I told them all pretty plainly that she was playing a game, that she wanted to ensure she was going to be locked up in a crazy house and this was how she would pay the deposit. She was intelligent enough to ensure her journey would take her to a place where she would feel more at home than she did in the real world.

It was down to me, a city tour guide at the time, to tell lawyers and doctors and judges that Mim was seeking to create the ultimate front. I told them she was seeking to deflect everything through the creation of an impenetrable hiding place in among a billion conversations, within a long con raised from the noise of her own unwell mind.

And all they could say was that, whatever I thought, there was no doubt she was a high-level psychotic, quite possibly in a constant state of hallucination.

'Yes,' I said, 'she is also very crafty and none of you see it.'

Ultimately my view counted for nothing. She was taken out of the criminal prosecution system and passed to the brave new just completed, Disneyfied-world of New Ready House. She was perfect material for its light-touch, fake freedom custody for the catastrophically deranged. They were, I was told, delighted to get her.

Anyway. Here we are, another hour-long stretch, another ring slipped around my neck to see what I can see.

'Did she see you?'

'...*raining you clunkette Sunday soup loud ad for cotton buds carpet's werecked last thing on earth I care about is what's said on LinkedIn fuck da masses uppa musical us to ensure that all 23x70 will fit...*'

As her own mother said, the bigger the front, the bigger the back.

'Did she see you?'

Did She See You?

> *'...more chance banshee hiccups call Weds and known symptoms spot...'*

If I'm going to write this book then everything goes in. To make my feelings clear, I'll have to say things no one knows. I'll have to say about the shop dummy. It had been used for a history display at Belfast City Hall and was hidden in my car as a joke by people I worked with. They'd dressed it up, pulled a balaclava over its head, put it in the boot knowing it would shock the shit out of me at some point. Well, it did. And I put it in the shed.

A few months after the murder I remember, in an act of massive drunkenness, I brought that thing into the house to act out an attack on Mim. I was wasted a lot in those days, often toying with the nasty fantasy of ending Mim's life because it briefly made me feel better. I played with the idea of smuggling a razor blade into New Ready House, of slashing her throat, of unzipping that scrawny neck all over the place as she sat there telling me about *'wardrobe essentials'* and how *'Bridget's gone for butter.'*

I'll write how I had practised that for a few blurred days. It was only through hard words and self promises that I hammered my mind back together.

But I'll not be showing anyone that mannequin. It's sitting on my living room sofa right now. It's still there in jeans and T-shirt, neck all war-gamed to death, androgynous throat slit twenty times. Don't break into my house if you don't want to scream. Don't freak out if you see me sitting beside some lean and cold individual with a bombed-out neck. But, as the shrinks have told me, I'm to be forgiven my moments of madness.

The gun that killed Fiz came from an ex-cop, a friend of her family. Roddy used to call around, look in on us, ask about Mim. It seemed obvious to me he was checking up, reporting back to her clan, telling them if he thought Mim was getting worse or better, if Fiz was well or not, if I was a good guy or not. They never knew as much as they wanted to know about me, but her people aren't what you might call friendly.

Roddy had been an intuitive interrogator, spent his career getting under the skin of gunmen captured from the armed factions of the Troubles. He had long been friends with Fiz's dad, a silent, thuggish-looking man who'd been some kind of gangster/ideologue crossover in his day. The story was, Fiz said, that the pair worked together, that Roddy protected her father's various interests while her father passed information to Roddy.

So, for whatever reason, after our crazy little family formed, Roddy felt it was his duty to 'pop in,' say 'hi' and have a look around now and then.

I'll say in the book how it makes me smile to know Our Trouble had the measure of him pretty fast, to remember how she put on her most inscrutable visage when he stopped by. Roddy's mind was full and busy when he was at ours, weighing all of us up, preparing his report for her kin. On that last occasion his brain got so busy he never noticed his backpack opening, his loaded personal protection weapon sliding out, the backpack closing again.

Fiz died four and a half hours after he left the house. Roddy had not even noticed the weapon missing. It was Mim's madness that killed Fiz, but Roddy and his gun paved the way.

'...in original packs and not downloads in the key mucker disappointed no further action peanuts tube station midnight are taking place for what...'

Did She See You?

'Did she see you?'
'...to see before agreeing and is recyclable suggest using November Keith taigs and web with sound on down to the lake of fear...'
'Did she see you?'
'...cabal and chip the key saving working group to address issue body tells your story all other simplicity is the ultimate elegance...'

Ten

Affirm: Memento mori.

I'M leaving the office and there's a card in the lobby mailbox. One red envelope sandwiched between flyers about road maintenance, bad water, cheap cheese and Wi-Fi. Beautiful calligraphic penmanship on front. I'm stunned, holding it now like a picture as a guy with a camera on his helmet passes by, as a woman inside a headset wipes tears and listens.

I go back into the office, open the blinds and sit down. I've never had a card before.

Maybe from Liam? The middle-aged accountant who needs to be more assertive after being passed over for promotion by a boss who has not spoken to him for a year? Or Jasmin? The actress who needs to be less impulsive after getting four bees tattooed on her face? Or Cassie the Heels? The depressed grandmother who needs to stop obsessing about her fitness and writing love letters to dangerous prisoners?

A many-coloured 'SO...' on the front. Inside, the black nib has swirled and swooped through the sumptuous whiteness.

'Denis.
Coffee?
I have an idea.
Thanks.
Bet (GoodShotForABlindGirl).'

Bet who drinks energy. What on earth does she want? What idea? I'm nothing to do with her, she's nothing to do with me. Wait. Is this her way of asking for a date? Why would she want a date? Why send a card and not an email? I made it clear to her I was a bit of a challenge via my reply, didn't I? I mean, I have Barbie Doll hair and a weird accent and tragedy all over me.

I am a desired man and I feel like a man who is desired.

I'll get an email address from her website and tell her I don't have time to meet.

The book will have some stuff about how Fiz liked to write letters and cards and little notes. She'd leave Post-its on the fridge, in the bed, on my toothbrush. I'd find those things in my pockets, my wallet, my overnight bag. Little tributes, little sparkles, little tantrums, little wishes, little explosions. They'd be in my shoes, on my car seat, in the laptop when I opened the cover. She'd think ahead about when and how she wanted to say things or reinforce things.

'Hang for you x.'
'Surprise!'
'Men who leave socks behind the sofa have a higher chance of dying before they turn 40.'
'Imagine a world where it was just us.'
'Due diligence!'
'I don't want to talk with you.'
'Dick.'
'My gran's birthday! Again!'
'I know you call the wee one Our Trouble but I will not give up.'
'My family are good people. Back off.'
'So you persist and I persist and on and on we run.'

I never chucked a single one, instead keeping them in a drawer like receipts of moments.

'I love you because you pause instead of exploding when you have been driven to the point of insanity.'

'I love you because you love me and that you know she is part of me and I swear I will never strike you again.'

'We cannot change her, but we can get better at surviving her and she might not be for their world but she is for our world.'

'She is a danger to herself but not to you or me and if you believe that you know you can leave so do not play that card.'

It's been four years since we took that break. The three of us, our first and last family holiday. We went to Florida then on to Jamaica. I hired a car in Florida, a convertible, roof down as we drove the hot Overseas Highway from Miami to Key West. Mim sat in the back chatting to herself, filming the road. The sun was fat, the wind was clean, the music was rich, our path clear.

I'd reached under my car seat, pulled out a small red box, handed it to Fiz.

'Look inside,' I said.

She'd no idea.

It had every note she'd penned over all the years. But now, stapled to each, my response.

'I know.'

'I'm sorry.'

'I will get better.'

'In a million years, I could never find a better partner than you.'

'My eye rolls express awe and wonder - your family is fascinating.'

'I told her you weren't happy and I gotta say she was kinda terrified.'

'Do you mind if I get a tattoo of your gran?'

'That tattoo would not last as long as your gran...'

Did She See You?

She was laughing, making her way through them one by one. There was a final note taped to the floor of the box which was to be the surprise, the point of it all.

A little hand appeared, Mim's little hand. It reached between the seats, grasped the edge of the box, yanked it from Fiz's hand. Fiz tried to grab it back, called out, 'No Mim,' but it was too late. Our Trouble had flung the box through the sunroof. Hundreds of little paper pieces were sent scattering - Fiz's thoughts, my thoughts, all spinning and sailing like word confetti among zooming traffic. The box hit the freeway, split open, lid sent flying. Cars, SUVs, trucks, crushing it to nothing. I'd jammed the brakes. A crazy move. We'd skidded right into the hard shoulder, painted rubber on the hot blacktop. Fiz'd lost it. She was shouting and roaring above the car horns. She screamed, *'You bitch!'* and her noise was everywhere, vivid, mighty, scary.

I was saying, 'Okay, okay, it's okay Fiz, okay, okay, okay.'

That was the only time I saw that level of anger in Fiz towards Mim. She fully lost it, just for a moment, and ultimately the whole episode ended up nesting in her mind, hurting her more than it ever troubled Mim.

For her part, Mim curled up on the back seat, started talking, hiding. Fiz, packed with adrenalin, wanted to get out, to stop the traffic, run around collecting the bits up. But that was futile, pointless, lethal. I put a hand around her arm, held it firm, watched her ball her fists and fight the urge to punch the car, Mim, me. I said, 'It doesn't matter. It doesn't matter. It doesn't matter.'

I'll be sure to write how Fiz was all I wanted, all I needed. We had love that made us feel lucky and certain. But she's gone, left with her raucous accent and fearless heart and that part of my life is over.

I need to get the direction right for the rest of my days now. I don't mind if it turns out loveless from here on, I just need it to be functional, material. If I was my client, I'd tell myself to do the same.

But that loose end, that last moment, has me tied tight, strapped into an emotional bind that won't let me make the final break. Fiz was so in touch with her senses, so receptive to her environment, to any information around her and I need to know what details she had at the killing point.

What I ask of Mim is simple, reasonable, understandable. It's just a binary fact, just a yes or no. Either Fiz's days ended without her even knowing, or her days ended with colossal horror. One is perfect, one is unbearable. Mim knows she can end this.

And I'm looking at my fingers on the keyboard now. I'm saying *Hey Bet* and *I'm sorry about the misunderstanding* and saying *I've not been thinking straight for a while*. I'm saying *I'm very busy but we'll meet sometime soon I'm sure*.

PS: Thanks for the snail mail, makes a nice change.

I move the cursor back up to her name and put in brackets after it *GoodShotForABlindGirl*, just to acknowledge the in-joke.

It's been going around in my head a lot, that line. Good shot for a blind girl. Did I see it somewhere or just invent it myself? Part of me thinks Bet did have it as her username but changed it after reaching out to me. Either way, why would it stick in my head? Does it mean what I think it means?

That other one does the same, that other line. Did she see you? Sometimes it takes on a life of its own. It's

Did She See You?

been hanging around my head so long, getting called up and deployed over and over again that it's got a little hangout of its own in this brain. It's a live thing, unresolved, always on like a flashing light or running tap. I've had these dreams about it, the words all over me, climbing the walls, rolling over the floor, all over Fiz as she lies there with that exit in her head.

Did she see you?

Right now it's like that again, like it's climbed out of my mind, is sliding down my arms, onto my hands, my fingers, onto the keyboard.

I'm watching my fingers play and this is nothing to do with Bet but I keep writing the question at the opening of this email - *'Did she see you? Did she see you? Did she see you? Did she see you?'* and I've done it twenty times and I can't send this email now but *I can handle everything because I am a high value alpha male.*

And I stop, sit back, say out loud, 'What am I doing?' I say, 'What the hell am I doing?' and try to take stock of this new situation.

I lean forward and think maybe this is grief or guilt and how it is important everyone takes responsibility for everything. I press send and get my coat and get up to go to the event and a scheduled message arrives from myself saying *Assert: The only easy day was yesterday.*

He wears this long yellow shirt like it's a dress. He's got white shorts like it's hot outside. He's got white flip flops, long dreadlocks, gold on every finger. He's got a twirly Hercule Poirot moustache, an unbuttoned waistcoat, two changes of footwear docked at the side of the stage.

'I do a lot of walking, man,' he says. 'I'm walking side to side of this stage and back again and I'm delivering all this wisdom and my feet get tired.'

Everyone's laughing, some clapping, some whistling. The online sensation who goes by the name HWKC Roundly has been rendered live in the flesh. He's a rock star, a warrior touring Europe to kick ass and sell books every lunchtime. His confidence is palpable, unstoppable, fiercely contagious.

He points, goes, 'In thirty minutes I'm gonna put on those big boots over there, okay? See them big boots? Get me some comfort.'

He opened to drumbeats, to a guitar riff he played himself as he strolled on stage. He started by saying everyone should admit they're both wrong and right, weak and strong, bad and good, and how it's a law of nature that you can't be one without being the other, you can't be great without being shit, that the shittier you are the greater your potential. He said these truisms are all linked to his big plan for world peace, a plot that boils down to getting people with opposing views to sit down and argue each other's case and I think he's serious.

He said, 'Argue your enemy's points TO your enemy. Do this with vigour. Do it until you understand your enemy's case so well he or she screams right in your face, "Hell yeah baby, you got it!"'

HWKC Roundly said, 'Then your enemy does the same. HE argues YOUR game. He fights YOUR corner. He counteracts whatever YOU raise against it to the very best of his ability. You get me? He is a warrior for YOUR case, YOUR cause, against himself. And when you find yourself just aching to clap your hands and scream out, "Preach it!" to the man you were fightin' then you

Did She See You?

KNOW you're at the place you needed to be. Closed-ended argument, my friends. Argument that closes when you are SATISFIED that your OPPONENT has put your case as well as you would like to put it yourself. These are the conversations between enemies that go somewhere. These are battles OUTSIDE the echo chamber. Everyone gets schooled, you know? Yeah. This is my mission, my friends.'

    He walks in holy silences, strolls that stage among random *whoops* from retail staff and frustrated chefs, goes, 'Enemies do not change each other's minds by doing their enemy stuff. No sir. They just become better enemies.

    'What enemies need to do is flip, right? And as you know, I do love flipping. You know what flipping does? It sheds light. Just like you flipped over a rock. It lets sweet light in. Bring everything into the light, my friends. If there's one message you take home from me today, it's – FLIP. IT. OVER.

    'So you like my shoes? You like these things they call flip-flops? I'm gonna take these off in a little while, gonna put on those boots and do some walking, right? When I'm done walking, right? I'm gonna tuck my toes into those slippers right there, you see them? That's when you know I'm wrapping it all up, when I'm getting ready for my HWKC Roundly siesta. You know?'

    I see Dagny. Or at least what looks like the back of her perfectly round, small head. I'm not certain it's her, can't be certain from this angle, but if she's still in town she'd likely be here. It's a bright blonde head I'm looking at. The last time I saw Dagny's head, about a week ago, it was blue. Before that, burgundy. The perfect shape of it, the symmetry, the sense of a thick neck. She's all squeezed between a suited pair upfront.

She's there as I'm leaving the hall, a white dot with a backpack disappearing and reappearing among mechanics and singers as she comes downstairs surrounded by people ready to argue each other's case.

I watch through the window as she stops outside, breaks off to pull a chequered green and purple hoodie over her face, to push those big mirrors back over her eyes. It's definitely her. I move with the crowd through revolving doors, look to my left, break off, press my way through puffed out chests.

I've been rude to Dagny and it didn't have to be that way. Right now I'm feeling sorry for her. I can at least say something. She's straightening the backpack, looking up as I arrive. The bottom lip is swollen badly on one side, a little chunk of flesh cut out of her chin. Looks like a car crash, a fall. I can't work out how there's so much violence in her life.

I say, 'Still here then, Dagny O'Reilly?'

She gets the pack straight, flashes a tiny smile, goes, 'Excuse me,' walks off.

I follow.

'Dagny,' I say behind her, 'let's try it? Argue each other's case?'

I'm beside her now.

'Walk fast for a short person,' I say.

'Small not short,' she says.

'Get a coffee with me. Please.'

'Why?'

'Just. It feels right. Maybe we can apologise to each other.'

'I don't need you, Denis.'

'Not asking to be on your show.'

Red man at the pedestrian crossing. We stop among forty or fifty of the newly coached. Twenty

Did She See You?

hands or more rise up, all holding the highest tech, all unlocking and swiping and scrolling.

She goes, 'I couldn't act like you.'

I say, 'Why not?'

She goes, 'I couldn't even play a character that dumb.'

And I don't know why I'm not troubled by her words. I seem to be in a great mood for some reason.

I tell her, 'I could argue as you. I'd be all positive, disruptive, challenging, resilient, annoying. Not sure I could dye my hair a different colour every day.'

'The last part's the most important part. My hair's my contribution to the beauty of the world.'

We drink coffee and she shows pictures of her Irish wolfhound, Dermot.

'He has an Irish accent when he barks,' she says, putting the phone away.

I say, 'No he doesn't.'

'Yeah. It's like instead of going 'arr arr arr' he goes 'aaarfy aaar aaar.' Don't laugh, I'm serious, man.'

'No doubt,' I say, and I think she is.

She goes, 'What's the weirdest thing in your home?'

'What?'

'You wanted to talk. We're talking. What's the weirdest thing in your home?'

She takes a short drink, a quick, functional kiss of the skinny latte.

I say, 'I have a dummy. I sit beside it sometimes. On the sofa.'

'A dummy?'

'Yeah. Like a shop dummy.'

'Like a mannequin?'

'Yes.'

'Has it got a face?'
'Faceless, you could say.'
'Weird.'
'It was a weird question.'
She goes, 'Yeah but it's creepy, dude. Why would you have that?'
'Long story.'
'Is it a sexual thing? You and the mannequin?'
'What? No.'
'I don't care if it is,' she says.

Her flight leaves in 'a couple of days,' she says. She's still got things to do, people to meet, places to see, she says. She's never been out of the USA before. She wants to build up a raft of material while she's here, stuff to use over the coming months.

I ask, 'What happened to your face?'
'Why are you asking about my face?'
'Every time I see you it has a different mark. There's a bruise on your forearm too. It's like you've been in a fight.'
'I bruise easy.'
'Someone hit you?'
'Why would someone do that?'
'Not the question.'
'Not your business.'
'Okay.'

She scoops foam from her coffee, puts it to her split lip. I feel like putting the mirrors on to match all the hiding, remind her what it's like to talk to someone with no eyes.

I'm about to say that and she goes, 'Put them on. I don't give a shit.'

It stuns me for a second, but she reads body language well.

Did She See You?

I go, 'How about you take those off?'

She shrugs. A little hand goes up, slips her mirrors off. Underneath, little green gems shine, the sparkling hearts of two black eyes.

'Holy shit,' I say, and she ignores it. And I was sure those eyes were blue.

She goes, 'Say things. Speak your mind. Let's talk, Dense Bic.'

'I've got a theory.'

'Tell me your theory.'

'I think you punch yourself.'

And she doesn't register it.

She says, 'Go on.'

I say, 'I think you've been getting your mind clear while you're away from home. I think you're reassessing. You're thinking *"What the hell am I doing with my life?"* I reckon you're lying in your hotel bed, eyes open, as your brain plays out this awkward stuff about who you are, where you're going, what you've done.'

And she's giving nothing away, so I go further, say, 'You put on a great act, Dagny. But I can imagine you sitting in front of the mirror wondering if you're on the right path. I think you're sitting there stuffing your face all alone at night. And then I imagine you punching the shit out of yourself. I think you're banging your hands and arms off the walls, hoping the rough reality of it all will somehow kick away all that bullshit floating around in your life.'

She touches the scrape on her chin, the little fleshy pothole.

I say, 'Millions out there thinking you have a perfect life, that you're the coolest thing on Earth. And you know it's not true. You can't tell them that, you could never explain it to them. They wouldn't understand it anyway. So you just keep on being the character you created a long time ago. But it means you can't grow, can't change. They don't want you to grow and it's getting you down. So now you're exploring. You're dressing it up as work, but really, it's for you, not them. That's why you're interested in my story. You want a piece of it just for a little dalliance with danger, a little vicarious living because it's less boring than being the same old Dagny every day.

'And it's not my story that takes you, is it? It's Mim's story. Young woman turns on the world, takes definitive action, becomes her true self in the most astonishing way. And to you, to this confident creation called Dagny O'Reilly, that strikes such a chord now. It's a reach but I'd say you've thought about extreme actions too. And I'm willing to bet...'

She butts in, goes, '...I'm willing to bet you have, as you might put it, taken the Red Pill. I'm willing to bet you were all plugged into the manosphere, loaded yourself up with crap about psychopaths having the right idea, about killing your niceness, all those assholes selling each other courses about stoicism and game.

'And I bet you loved it, learned it, took it to its ironic conclusion and dropped offline because now you think online has no authenticity. You dropped the fake to live the real as you seek to make money, make enemies, build muscle, be all high value alpha. I've looked at all this stuff too, Denis. I know the kind of character it attracts.'

I go, 'I'm just trying to move on.'

And we pause, blood warm, tails up. I look around, see who might be tuned into this indelicate reduction,

Did She See You?

this jabbing scrutiny of ours. Quiet coffee house phone enthusiasts are everywhere, silently selecting emotions as we talk.

Dagny goes, '*Non magni pendis quia contigit.* Latin. I bet you can translate.'

I'm smiling because she's right.

I go, '*One does not value that which is easily obtained.*'

'Damn straight,' she says. 'And shit like that has you swimming hard and talking tough and, you know, putting on this character of yours. You lie in bed and consider how liberating it is to know the great truth is you are truly alone in this world. You've learned no one gives a shit about anyone else and it's useful to you.

'You know, don't you Denis, that people care what you have to offer them but not about you? This stuff's become important. It comes from your ordeal as a parent to that crazy freak. I'm guessing Fiz felt the same. I'm guessing she felt that way first, that you learned from her. And when you lost her, you tipped head-first into what made sense to her because she was your truth, your rock, the only reason you hung around.'

It's a cold, clear audit. If she was my client, I'd have won her over for months. If I was hers, I'd be back again and again.

She says it quietly now, 'The world is filling up with bullshit, isn't it? Humanity has peaked, hasn't it? It's got so high that now there's crack after crack in the edifice and a common fall is coming. Politics, identity, law, pop culture, consumerism, food, parenting, relationships, sex, gender, disease control, the planet itself, all going to shit. It's always been about progress up to now, and we've made it, we damn well worked out how to fix the world and thought we'd ended history.

'But then we got all hooked on comfort and sat around designing new battles because comfort doesn't make us alive.

'We're sitting in panic rooms tweeting the shit out of ourselves, wrapping ourselves up in useless balms and talking about the quality of our depression and anxiety and gender and craving disruption and conflict.'

I cannot help but smile, saying quietly, 'Jesus Dagny.'

She goes, the whole place listening, 'All the great ideas were in the old books, weren't they Denis? Those guys would have hated where we are now – all of us like fat, scared sheep in concrete fields. Turns out, Denis, freedom's wasted on the free.'

And I don't know why but I feel proud of her as she goes, 'So you've stepped away because you know a level of discomfort is necessary for the human to function properly, for nature itself to proceed. We all NEED a problem, don't we Denis? We all need a fight, a cause, a victory to chase.

'Struggle is good, right? People come out of cancer wards ten times the people they were when they went in. People who go to war, who starve, who crash, come back nothing less than upgraded. It's why we climb sheer cliff faces, ride motorbikes at 200mph.

'Nothing grows in the comfort zone, Dense. Not one thing. It's why we test ourselves over and over, to discover the struggle, to learn the eternal lessons that the smartest minds knew in the simplest times. You know all this now because you've faced struggle, you've faced something hard and uncompromising. Did it break you? No. It is on its way to making you.

'There is a constant war going on, isn't there? And you can either decline and eat, sleep and jerk your way

Did She See You?

through it, or you can ascend. Your grief sent you in search of meaning because so much meaning was taken from you. And look how far you've come. You are incoming fire now Denis Bic, in everything you do, everything you are. And incoming fire, my friend, has the right of way.'

And she's done.

I'm laughing and thinking 'how does she know I go swimming?' but it would be churlish to ask right now.

She goes, 'One other thing I want to mention.'

And I'm laughing, saying, 'What's that?'

She goes, 'Her family say you lied about everything.'

Jason Johnson

Eleven

Assert: In silence I hear others' imperfections and conceal my own.

TUNES low, gears high, driving to meet Bet. Feels good streaming along this motorway all confident that whatever I'm going to say to this woman will be enough.
I expect nothing because I always expect nothing.
I check the mirror, press back into the seat and say *'Dinggggg'* from the back of the throat, say *'Dongggg'* from deep in the neck and hold it to enrich the voice.
I push my foot now and my mind gets me this memory of Mim's leap from that taxi in Jamaica, finds one of her scattering notes in Florida. My mind asks me to consider the car was the common denominator in those incidents as if rushing along somehow compelled her to act. I think how we never move now, that I'm the guy on repeat in the same place, a mouth on a chair saying the same thing twice a week. I think how Our Trouble holds the cards, holds all the power in the ever-upgraded place where she lives. It's me who some might say is the mad one now, it's me repeating the same thing and expecting a different result.
We need a change of scenery. I need to talk to Mim somewhere else. I need to ask her the same thing somewhere else. I need to interrupt the pattern, try for a different result.
I say, 'Christ,' shake my head. I force my foot down and sail off the slip road, speed along the main route into town with my white hair and bottled scent. Sometimes it's like I could just drive forever, drive through the night and morning like they're just places

Did She See You?

to pass. If there was a road, a highway lapping the whole world, a belt around the equator, I'd drive it until my hair turned black, until my skin pooled around me. I'd never stop, never bump the sides, a single direction to sate the mind.

I'll be telling readers how I had a job as a tour guide at Belfast City Hall. Then, when I knew I could sell a sense of excitement, I got a job telling people what they wanted to hear about The Troubles. I'd talk urgently about the way locals sing of skinny little broke guys from along the road who killed skinny little broke guys from along the road. I'd ride the bus with them, show clients where bombs went boom, say how the lights flashed on and off. I'd say how those bombs tore off ears and feet and jawbones, that they rammed bedrock grime and steel into limbs. I'd talk about funerals and pubs and say headstones get pissed on in acts promoted to fair in the many-fronted bloody pantomime of neighbourhood war. We'd gawk at invisible boundaries spammed by paint and flags, at peace line streets where people cannot face each other. I'd accept their tips and tell how I'd been the outsider at ceremonies of attention, the new face in places where facts clash and fractions of identity become binary wholes.

It's means justify ends here, I'd say, just cause and effect here, I'd say. There are no wonders here, no successes here, no golden silence or divinity got built here, I'd say. I'd tell them it's just punishment and reward, remedy and failure, long knives and bandages and it all just has its own rise and fall, its own heavy heart beating away.

This son of a far-off civil war was here telling a new old story, here scraping words out of songbooks, here rubbing oil on sexy distortions in the way every other guy in the sales game does. I'd have American professors hanging on every word, Aussie porn stars pondering if they know anything at all, foggy army veterans and ex-fugitives asking for help piecing together their losses and gains.

They liked talking to me, hearing my take on the way cracked things lean on themselves. And when I came to know which well-dressed bit-truths became whole truths, I told them again.

Bet's arrived before me and I'm twenty-four minutes early. She's drinking, slumped in a hotel bar armchair and looks like she's been there all day. A black tee, logo on the sleeve. A single tattoo, just a few neat words on the upper right arm. There's white jeans, a black shapeless pendant on black cord. The short blonde hair has a blood-red clip holding the side part. She's scratching her face, staring at the wall, all unimpressed and expecting nothing.

I don't know why I agreed to this, don't know why I said yes when she assured me she would not waste my time because I don't like this already.

I go, 'Bet' and my voice sounds like a squeak.

She goes, 'Denis. How are ya?'

She undoes the slump, stands strong. We do this little elbow bump.

She goes, 'What're you having?'

I look at her glass, the crimson, the ice, that viscous fizz.

I say, 'You on the Red Bull?'

She nods, 'Of course. With vodka. Fuck society. Want one?'

'Yes. No vodka.'

Did She See You?

'No vodka?'
'I don't.'
'You serious?'
'Yeh. The mistress of success requires your bad habits as payment and all that.'

She walks to the bar, puts bare elbows on polished oak and I'm watching her sea swimmer's form and thinking we could skinny dip in the shipping lane.

Bet returns with a swagger, composure solid. We drink energy and chat.

She says, 'I have my own history, right?'
'What do you mean?'
'Just stuff. Like attracts like and all that.'
'Okay.'
She goes, 'How many clients have you got?'
'Twenty.'
More like five.
She takes a slug, goes, 'You've made a success.'
'I suppose.'
'All inside, what, eighteen months or so?'
'How many do you have?'
'Five. What's your secret?'
'If there's a secret, Bet, it's the back story. Hate to think people are drawn to me because my wife was shot in the head, but people are drawn to me because my wife was shot in the head.'

'People are shit, as you know. They don't care about your wife. They'd ask for selfies if they could get away with it.'

I go, 'It's true. But I'm good at what I do. That's how I hang onto them.'

'Your most interesting client?'

I let the sticky drink mould around my gums, sink my teeth into it, feel it biting back.

112

I go, 'I've a woman who was told by a judge to get a life coach. Some charity funds it. Relentless kleptomaniac, zero confidence. I hide the valuables before she arrives.'

'Who else?'

'A bipolar trying to get a grip after finding out her partner's very special love for foodstuffs.'

'Yeah,' she goes, 'there's some weird food stuff going on out there. Not traditional coach material but for some reason they come to us. An appointment with us is not an admission you have a problem. I get the fatties and skinnies and addicts too. Regular income.'

'We're like priests at confession, I think. Identifying sins, dishing out punishment.'

'So why call yourself a "mercenary life coach"? I read it on your website. It's infantile.'

'Infantile?'

'Yes.'

'I use words that appeal to people who want something else. Men, mostly. If they're the lonely sort, I tell them they can become a wolf. If they're angry, I say they can use it to fight. Mercenary, sovereign, warrior – all trigger words.'

'What you're saying is that your target market is assholes?'

'Still a market. Do you know what the Red Pill is?'

'Like from The Matrix?'

'Yes. That's all part of my niche. What I offer contrasts with all that social justice warrior stuff, all that virtue signalling, that internet noise. Mercenary just about says all of the above.'

She goes, 'I drink too much,' and I don't know why she said that. She goes, 'You have the right idea.

Did She See You?

Imminent plans to upgrade, you see. And once I commit to a thing, I see it through.'

'Are these plans what you wanted to talk about?'

'Yes,' she says, and that glass is empty.

You want another one of those things?'

'Yeh. A double. I like getting pissed. At least for now.'

I go, 'Fine.'

Just as I'm standing, she goes, 'I'm so sorry about your wife.'

And it's like a punch in the belly, a kick in the balls and I can say anything in the world I want to say now. I'm thinking how she's had a few already, that she was here a while before I showed. I'm thinking all that and staying calm and thinking I must have misread her.

I go, 'Okay. Thanks.'

'And did you see it happen?'

'I think you know the answer. Do you want ice?'

'Your daughter-'

'-step.'

'Right. Stepdaughter. She was right in front of you?'

'Why are you asking?'

'It's good to confront these things, right?'

'On my own terms, if you don't mind.'

'Work with me.'

'Why? You said you had a question to ask me. Don't tell me that was it?'

'No. And I do. I promise. But I want to know a little more about you first.'

'About me or the murder of my wife?'

'You didn't have a chance to stop your stepdaughter?'

'You want to know how come I didn't save my wife's life?'

'Just want a feel for how it happened. It's helpful for me. I mean, there were lots of press reports, but never a court case to get to the detail of the whole thing. They just locked that crazy kid away in New Ready House, as far as I know.'

I could just walk away. She has turned this into something it was never meant to be.

I go, 'You either get drunk quick or you've been here all day.'

'Neither.'

'So this is you sober?'

'Almost. Is that bad?'

I sit back down, lean forward, look into her pretty, hard face.

I say, 'If you know anything about this case, you'll know it broke me. Why would you ask me this stuff?'

She goes, 'Because it's the right thing for us to talk about. Because we're both moving forward, both islands of honesty in the middle of an honesty famine, Denis. Because we're friends and colleagues, aren't we?'

I go, 'No. You're less of a person than I thought.'

'I'm more.'

I go, 'I don't think so.'

'You're judging me on a question I asked? The guy with the bleached hair and matching belt is judging me so quickly?'

'Oh, I think you're the one judging.'

'I don't want to judge you, Denis. I want to challenge you. Don't you ever want to be challenged? Can we not challenge each other?'

'I have no idea who you are and you want to challenge me to talk about the murder of my wife?'

Did She See You?

'Wasn't murder though, was it? Not technically. It was the killing of your wife by someone with diminished responsibility. Right? You saw that girl aiming at your beautiful wife and you stood and watched her shoot. Good shot for a blind girl, eh?'
'Fuck you,' and I'm going.
'Wait.'
'No.'
'The reason.'
'Fuck the reason.'
'It's a business idea. Your background is important.'
'What business idea?'
'You and me in business together. That's what I wanted to talk to you about.'
'Not interested.'
She lays her open palms in front of her, fingers spaced, looks up. She wriggles the fingers, beckons me, beckons my hands.
'Trust me,' she says.
'I don't even like you.'
'I don't care if you like me, Denis.'
She wriggles the fingers again and I'm too curious not to do what she wants. I put my hands in hers. She squeezes them, closes her eyes, opens her eyes, selects one. I pull my left hand back and she has both her hands, bare, ringless, unpainted, on my right. She leans in, smells it, the fingertips, the palm. She pulls it along, under her nose, breathing in for longer than you'd think she could.
She goes, 'You can tell a lot about a person...,' and breathes in again, smells the wrist, between the fingers, '...by smelling their hands.'

I feel her nose now, the little round tip ploughing along the folds, some weird reading ceremony, some fad beloved by cloudy-brained rude people who down energy drinks.

I say, 'I see.'

She goes, 'I'm going to tell you things about you.'

And she pauses for a second, maybe for effect, and I can't hold off.

I say, 'Hair gel, soap, maybe some Rattle Head – that's the name of my aftershave. Maybe mint because I ate two before coming here.'

'There's something distinctive I can't identify.'

I smile, shake my head, say, 'You're so full of shit.'

She goes, 'Just information gathering.'

I take my hand away. She puffs her face out, cheeks filling fast.

I go, 'You okay?'

She opens her mouth, a kind of satisfied gasp. A strange kind of fish-like trait she has there, some kind of tell.

She goes, 'Rattle Head doesn't exist.'

'True.'

'And you didn't eat any mints.'

'Correct.'

'You've been swimming recently.'

'Correct.'

'Somewhere grimy.'

'Correct.'

'Your car has a faux leather steering wheel.'

'I'm impressed.'

'Tell me the truth and I will never breathe a word.'

Twelve

Assert: Blowtorch your past and everyone in it – do not be afraid to rise.

    MY mother was offered a new life in someplace she'd never heard of 2,000 miles away when I was seven. We had been given the chance to escape a short, sincere war in our own land and she had to take it.
    I met Fiz at primary school here and, among all my learning of a new language, we became friends quickly. She said my skin and bones looked new, that she liked the way my accent had flashes of hers.
    She told me her gran Freda had smuggled guns around in prams when her children were young. She told me her dad Joe had been involved in the violence in the city and killed people. I said my father had been accused of lying by a Balkan war criminal and tortured to death with electricity and that real life's only wholesome in fractions. Fiz said her family had cars, houses, bouncers, drugs and money and I said mine had nothing.
    She had clenched fists and big earrings and a tongue of cash at every ATM. Her people were all 'connected' and had often shed blood for each other. She said she always thought she might one day need to die for them, that bold decisions, bloody stubbornness and dying were celebrated family traits. She said one cousin, Raymond, was planning to be a murderer as a career and that was okay. She told me one uncle, Stefan, was in jail for running a protection racket and he was well-liked. All of that anti-status, she said, afforded them respect in various corners of the local

underworld. It afforded them an extraordinary home too. The first time I saw her house I told her the hovel where my mother and I stayed would fit in its toilet and we'd laughed about that.

Our friendship turned into teenage dates, little fanfares, small adventures, and it was a hoot to kick around with her. She'd talk people out of bother, talk them into bother, be the key moving part of whatever event was fastest or funniest among the people and situations we knew. I was there when she had a fallout with a guy who groped her one time, gasped as she punched him in the face and he fell over.

Part of our deal in those days was we met and parted easily, went elsewhere with no drama. She didn't take it personally when her friend told her I'd taken her camping in the cold hills with a pizza, some drugs and a condom, and I loved her for that.

Fiz did great in school, went off to uni, sat a law degree. I'd never aimed high, more inspired by the boozy ways of people I fell in with. I ended up broke in Belfast, staying with my mother, sucking on spliffs secured from Fiz's freed cousin Raymond and thinking about a change in direction.

One time I bumped into Fiz and her gran Freda and we had this funny little hour where we all clicked, where the sweet old gunrunner said Fiz and I would make a great couple. Fiz and I hugged nice and tight. She had, she said, decided against a career in law and was rethinking life.

She dropped Freda off at her nursing home, came back to me. We spent the night in a B&B where people in the next room complained about our loud love. I asked her to marry me in the morning, over breakfast, among the stern faces and said I'd always known in my

Did She See You?

soul I'd found my true north, and it was a stupid thing to do. She wasn't sure what I was at when I took to one knee, ringless, after pouring her tea. I could see in her face there was some itch she couldn't scratch, some puzzle she hadn't solved, and I'd just made it all more complicated. Neither of us finished that breakfast. None of the other guests spoke. It was shit.

I confided the lot to my mother that night, said I was heaving with embarrassment. She was a sweet woman, riddled with cancer at the time. She gave me a ring she wore, said it was for 'the one,' that I would know when she came along and I got into the habit of taking that ring everywhere on a chain around my neck.

I lived the student life for a while, hooked up with Raymond and some other bad company and partied the shit out of myself some more. I watched my mother's cancer eat the last of her in hospital and held her hand as her honest eyes closed for the last time.

And the very next day Fiz approached to say she was sorry for everything. But she was wired, as messed up as I was trying not to be. She said the more time passed the more she kept thinking about us, about that mad morning at the B&B. She said she didn't understand where we went wrong, but that she'd made a mistake and I could barely make out her words.

She told me about going off the rails, falling in with a druggie crowd, said she wanted to fix it all. She was going to work in care, she said, to look after people to help set her compassion and empathy free. Many relatives had stepped away from her, she said. There was no one, she said. And she wanted no one but me, she said.

We sat on some steps and she wept, asked me if I had any plans for the rest of my life, asked me if I'd marry her. We hugged, held, slipped easily back into our own company once again. She whispered 'Yes' to me as our faces were pressed close and I knew what she meant.

    She was precious and pale and soft-skinned, some kind of beauty born from some wrongness back there in a world of guns and robberies and blood and bonfires. She was kind and easy going and badass all in one, had a thirst for intensity and knowledge that was almost physical, almost audible, and the more she learned about this world the harder she became. She was into teeth and flared trousers and tying her hair up. She had, when required, access to dirty money and bad people but never wanted much to do with any of it. She told me that day how the world was all lies and said I was the only honest person she knew. She took a ring from her pocket, said her dad, a police informer, had been raging against his world. She said demons had been spinning in his head, that he'd had a career built on lies and brutalisation and murder, that he had himself just been beaten to death in some bullshit power struggle. She said the ring belonged to him, that it had witnessed too much terror and said she'd been saving it for me because she wanted everything to change, to get better, and I understood what she was trying to say. I lifted the chain from my throat, showed her my mother's gift to mc.

    A few weeks later we broke up again. I'd asked her when we should think about getting married and she said she didn't want to anymore.

    I'd said, 'Go fuck yourself.'

    I hooked back up with Raymond and others among her shameless cousins, and wrote Fiz out of my life. Two months or more later she found me at the

Did She See You?

death of a day, bags packed and ready to leave mum's old flat forever, to catch a late plane and become a returning migrant to a now peaceful place I hardly knew. She was standing at the door just as I was going out.

    I said, 'Why are you here?'

    She said, 'I have to tell you something.'

    I said, 'What?'

    And she had this scar on her neck, this healed mark where violence had been. And there was this tooth that had changed, this eyelid that didn't sit as it used to.

    She breathed in long and I brought her in among the dark and this diamond of dull light from the street fell on her face and she said, 'I'm pregnant.'

    And it was like my central nervous system was seized by something and pulled through my skin because the way she said it was not the way anyone says that.

    'Okay,' I said, 'what do you want me to say?'

    'Nothing,' she said.

    'Whose?'

    Tears were coming and she dropped her head, said, 'I don't know.'

    And it was like every muscle was being shredded by wolves, like my vision was morphing from real to surreal, like my thoughts were falling apart as they formed.

    It was her way of telling me she'd been raped.

Jason Johnson

Miriam – Two of Three

SHE turns in air, light and twisting in the wakening, blazing sky, rocketing to earth.

The rush forces her face open, her eyes, her mouth, the wind splitting the seals of her skin and blasting inside. Her head's spun from within, neck cranked, the twist throwing her vision high.

Pelting through this storm could tear her limbs right off, could friction skin from her bones, could rip ears from her head, could blow these brains out into the dawn.

The tall building's right at her side, hanging from the heavens, fiery in the new day's flare.

A figure up there looking over a rail, the man in her room, his glassy face just a dot of orange. She's zooming down the long hotel and she passes written words like all its little bricks are named as she's spun head over heels.

A thump now, a thunderous crack as the big building itself seems to lose footing. A punishing crunch as the ground gives way and one whole hotel floor sinks, shaking, into the ground.

And another blast like the end of a world as another floor of the quaking tower gets piled into the bedrock. Then another, then another.

Rapid twirling, limbs flinging, arms and legs kicking, head shaking with the riot in her eardrums. The hotel crashing fast into the earth, chunk by chunk, floor by floor. And it's dashing into the ground beside her now like carriages on a train.

Motionless people in the windows, all facing her, all holding small machines at her, all filtering a girl in a hurricane as they plunge, blast by blast, alongside her.

Did She See You?

And she knows the shiny man on the balcony will be coming now, racing down alongside her.

She sees as he leaps from the edge, dives towards her as she falls. She sees bones inside sheer skin, opaque teeth gritted, mouth forming words her full ears can't hear and she knows he's calling, '...and you persist so I persist and on and on we run...'

And a loosened brick, like a lump of shrapnel from this out-of-control catastrophe, whooshes past, spirals end-to-end into the distance like a bad bullet and its word was 'run' and from nowhere she knows she'll say it. There's just a small blue pool coming closer now from below and she knows that word will be the last thing she'll ever say, that it was the first thing he had said. It'll be the only thing they ever share, all he ever has of her, and so, mouth full of blazing sky, she tries to say...

Vision gone.

And she's moving upwards now, the messy roaring returning to the ears as she's rising up through water, physics compelling her from the depth through which she crashed.

Her eyes open and it's like red smoke all around her, the blood of her own limbs billowing in the water, skin stripped from flesh, rare shapes of it swirling around, sticking to the wrong raw parts.

An inch from the top, an inch from a breath and his face is there, hanging still now over the surface of the water, white pupils set on her.

Invisible skin reveals veins like cords full and tight, a tongue gathering in his head as if to spit. The torso reveals the rise and fall of the ribs, the giving and taking of the heart. He hangs unmoving, his vile body coruscating, his skinless fingertips touching her face.

And once more, inaudible among the destruction, his face goes, 'So,' goes, 'so,' to heavy thumps of masonry into the ground, mouths, 'I persist so you persist and on and on we...?'

He turns his alien head on its neck, an ear and all its tiny bouncing bones and beating drum towards her now.

A maroon plume of her blood blossoms upwards from the wind-torn seams of her flesh. All is clouding over and he's holding, waiting for her to speak.

From under the water, she says...

Thirteen

Assert: Live as if already dead – without fear of the end point.

OUR Trouble is a little different today. A more assured performance than usual. The words are a little clearer.
'Did she see you?'
'*...red rocks in the sun so I took lots of pix move CG to Norm's place in the middle of our street quiche and the arrival was fun fun scoop out some of that one hundred you look amazing it was nothing xx terf barf toy story...*'
The search for patterns, for shifts in pitch and tone and pause, is an exacting task. Who could know what any of it means anyway? Yet there is, right now, something... else.
I'll write how the best thing about these visits is there's no small talk. There's no 'hello,' no chat about how her week has been. There are no updates on whatever meals have been served here. The chef's great, they say. The entertainment's relentless, apparently. The whole place is a holiday camp, some insist. But I give not one fig about any of that.
'*...virtue and pottery my vices floors what's your sort code heaven tits can go insipid arty get your mornings right face like a dunkelosteus ra will end WGTN if sally rods abseiling...*'
'Did she see you?'
There was a new pause there, a break in her train of thought, a fraction of a second longer than the mini-breaks I'm used to, right when I asked it. She's more present today. On whatever scale there is for these

things, she's playing her game one or two notches up from when I last saw her.

'Did she see you?'

'...fur in the oven or maybe Margaret's cooking walk in here with your stupid bag holy diver better dead off to the lake of fear red bricks yeh faith is a full stop feck aff cappuccino...'

Face straight and I whisper, 'You shot her in the head. You shot her in the head. You know you did. You shot her in the head. You shot her in the head. You killed the only person who ever loved you. You shot her in the head. Did she know? Did she know you killed her? Think of your mother, Mim. Did she know you killed her? Did she see you?'

'...say KAT steaming Arnie once more Lego bridge Phil's made his case for now you're a bean in a jar Mary nothing annoys more than words leaves are brown all stare at our shit gamble...'

She'd hold the world record for the most voices in a human head at the one time if she wasn't pretending. She'd be the most intricate case in history if she wasn't making it all up. Her brain's on relentless autopilot, seizing fast on every little word and phrase it can get.

'Did she see you?'

'...through smoke and mirrors np after all we joked colour TV infinity is insanity half a disaster swim gin o'clock cunt...'

'The moment you stop is the moment things change.'

'...raisins car park behind there channelling Buck Rogers enter a third time for free...'

'I can help you, get you anything you need in here. Just stop.'

Did She See You?

'...*silence among thistles get two drinks for Sean laminate is cheaper kids in America blizzards of happy...*'
'Did she see you?'
Only persistence will break her. Only non-stop will stop her. I'll be back again and again to this cuckoo's nest, back to park and target like a contender at the oche, firing these darts for as long as it takes.

I'll say in the book how I sat here once and told her the details of a car crash outside that didn't happen to see if she'd tune in. I told her once about a food poisoning emergency in the hospital that didn't happen. I told her Fiz left her a mansion in California in the will and how she'll be able to go and live in it if she stops talking. That was balls too.

But change is inevitable, is always underway, is always coming and always resisted. I've months of material to compare, dozens of hours of performance to rate and review. I hear, see, feel anything fresh, anything outside the pattern of what counts as her behaviour. I can't tell you what any of it means but I do believe any change, anything at all is positive. Any departure is progress.

'Did she see you?'
'...*reaching out to take my hand and I said no there isn't a thing I don't know about him blow-dry laminate he thinks he is guilty mustard or dog shit I can't tell...*'
'Did she see you?'
Does she get headaches from this madness? Does her jaw hurt? What if she lost her voice? Does she have a strategy, a way of coming up with it all? Does she picture any of the people in her head? Are there regular characters? Does she practise when she's alone? How many times has she tucked her hair, how many words has she said?

I got her a tinfoil hat once. I asked Dr Harriet to arrange it, to have foil brought to me one time I met her. She wasn't mad about the idea but sorted it out once she was sure it had nothing to do with drugs or suicide. I made a little cap for her, placed it on her head, wrapped it over her ears, told her it would all stop now, that the errant radio waves couldn't reach her brain now. She didn't get the joke.

I explained to Harriet that I'd wanted to do it to confirm she's receiving nothing through the air, to prove it's all already in her head.

Harriet went, 'You want to confirm it to me? What on earth gave you the impression I believe her? For the last time, Mr Bic, when I said she was phenomenal, I was NOT talking about her ability to receive messages. I was talking about her creativity and fortitude. You don't listen to me at all and I find that distressing.'

I explained –

Wait.

What was that?

She just looked up. Mim did. As far up as my neck. She ran a hand behind her right ear and as she brought it down, she looked towards me.

'Mim. Did she see you?'

'*...within the main building a soul in sight...*'

'Stop talking. Did she see you?'

'*...there isn't a thing I don't know about him...*'

Wait.

She's just said that '*...isn't a thing...*' thing for a second time. She's fluffed her lines. Something's going on in that head, something else. I'm right about this today, about something different. She's made room for something else in her mind and it's got in the way of her flow.

Did She See You?

'Did she see you?'

'*...untold in nero when obvious white lines milk you look amazing to four four why...*'

I go to Shadi at the front of the room. People look up, nod as I pass by. We're all the victims here, like mutual friends of the dead at a funeral here, all brothers and sisters with gutted lives.

'Shadi?'

'Denis.'

I'm quiet when I go, 'She's different. Not as evenly paced. Or something. Hard to say.'

'Okay.'

'What's changed? I mean, new drugs? Or what? Something's changed. Maybe just a little thing.'

He thinks, looks down, back to me, goes, 'Nothing I know of.'

'You sure? I mean, I know her, right? Better than anyone, I'd say.'

He shrugs, unable to help.

I look around his station - the documents, the soft-covered devices, the mobile phone part tucked under papers. I nod to the Samsung, say, 'She tried to steal that from you yet?'

'I'm sorry?'

'Your phone. She likes to film things. You know, little self-harming videos, little kicking cats videos or digging her fingers into the mud videos or singing crackpot song videos. You know that kind of thing?'

'She is artistic,' he says, and it's the nicest thing he could say about all of that.

'We got her one in the end,' I say, 'just so she could film stuff. Never connected her to Wi-Fi though. Turns out she had her own Wi-Fi in her head all along.'

I'm chuckling at my joke here. Laughs from the staff are hard to come by here.

He goes, 'She hasn't tried to steal my phone, Denis.' He looks up, a glint in his eye as he whispers, 'Maybe she is still working out a way to do it.'

It makes me smile.

I say, 'What's the position with taking her out? I mean, for a walk or even a drive somewhere. Could I ever do that? How does that stuff work?'

He goes, 'I'm not sure I understand.'

I say, 'Some people in here get out on different schemes and all of that, right?'

'Yes,' he says.

'And sometimes they can meet relatives or friends?'

'Yes. I think you should talk to Dr Harriet about all of that.'

I say, 'Okay. I just feel I'll be able to get more out of her if we change the scenery.'

He has this blank look as if I just asked him would it be okay for a devious murderous psycho to mingle among the public.

I say, 'I do see a change in her today, Shadi.'

'Yes, you said.'

'It's like something's shifted. Has her diet changed, or has she moved rooms? I mean, anything like that? Has she interacted with some...'

He knows something. His big clear eyes dive, head tips forward. There's something he's trying to bury.

'Shadi?' I say very quietly now, 'just between you and me.'

He shakes his head.

'Shadi. You and me. What is it?'

Did She See You?

He looks up, looks around, clears his throat a little, whispers, 'Maybe someone other than me told you this.'

I go, 'Of course. You did not tell me anything.'

He nods, accepts we understand each other, goes, 'Another visitor. That's all.'

'Seriously? Who?'

He shakes his head, looks as if to say he doesn't know, that he's said all he can.

And I'm thinking and going, 'What the hell? Shadi? I've a right to know.'

'I can't say because...'

In clear, firm whispers, I'm saying, 'Tell me. We agreed. I didn't hear it from you. Who visited? Tell me?'

He looks up once more, looks behind me at the visitors, at Mim. And it's coming, this response. Another tiny little grunt as he clears his throat - unusual traffic on the way.

Ever so quietly, looking down again as if I'm not there at all, Shadi goes, 'I can't say, I'm sorry. I honestly do not know who the person was.'

There have been no other visitors before. Mim was cut off like a rotten limb by Fiz's headstrong family. The rapist's daughter was outcast like a demon. I had to keep coming back, maybe not out of the goodness of my heart, but I had to keep coming back. Everyone else just entrusted her to the state and its endless patience, to the new cuckoo's nest with the green glowing doors and high-end shrinks. No one else could bear to be with her.

Then it hits me.

'Was it a woman, Shadi? A young woman. Was it a chubby American girl?'

His head shakes, eyes down.

'I don't know,' he says, 'I don't know.'

I say, 'Who?'

'No.'
'Who?'
'No, sorry.'
'It was Dagny O'Reilly, wasn't it?'

Fourteen

Assert: I win the fight when I'm first and fast and ferocious.

I TOLD Bet some things in that hotel bar. I told her to go away, to mind her own business and to never communicate with me again. In the car park, she told me she was so sorry, that she had misjudged everything, that she had drunk too much and hoped I could understand.

I told her Mim was being cared for, that there were drugs that gave her a baseline of contentment, that she was safe from herself. I told her I admire the staff, the institution itself, the endless patience of the state.

She came close and asked what hand I played in the sack, what ride I took between the sheets. She wanted to know if I was Carousel or Roll-O-Plane or Big Dipper or Log Flume or Ghost Train or Rollercoaster. She wanted to know who I was when the inhibitions went, what I'd ask if I could have it all. She wanted to know what words I'd use, what abbreviations I'd explore, where I'd be, what I'd be doing, what I'd be wearing if I was to go to bed with her.

I said, 'What are you talking about?'

She said, 'Sex. Are you nervous? Do I make you nervous, Denis?'

'A bit, yeah. What the hell's Roll-O-Plane?'

'You're not used to this, are you?'

'Flirting?'

'The dance. The woo. The tease.'

'It's been a while.'

'No one since your wife?'
'No.'
'Okay. Well, we'll see how we go.'
I went, 'What?'
She said, 'Let's date.'
I said, 'Not sure.'
She asked, 'Why did you email me that question?'
I'd forgotten.
I went, 'Oh that? Just a joke. Weird sense of humour.'
'Did *who* see me do what?'
I went, 'Bet, forget it.'
'No,' she said. 'I'll find out. I always find out everything in the end.'
'Whatever.'
'Your thing, your niche, is getting people ready for work, for conflict, for success.'
'Nicely put.'
'Have you done that for anyone wanting to fall in love?'
I thought for a moment and said, 'No.'
'You had a good marriage, as everyone knows. Until she was killed, dramatically, famously, infamously. Right?'
'Seriously?'
'Wait. The reason, right. You and I team up, okay? We're the coaches who will *boost your love life, help you get that date, fix your marriage?* We're the people who can get you to man up, to woman up, to hunt down whoever and whatever it is you want, to get whatever it is you want. We'll make you the hottest thing on the street and online, we'll pack you with confidence and gusto and make you irresistible. All in the name of

passion, sex, love. Single, couple, whatever. You look like you're going to yawn. Do you get what I'm saying?'

'Not sure. I was planning on driving home.'

'Sex and love and romance. Everyone has an interest in all of that. And just about everyone's relationship needs work. And that's not even counting all the incels lost to porn or the gamer refugees. It's the most recurring thing I hear - relationships. So why don't we meet the market, give it a shot? We'd get shit loads of publicity, loads of clients. I'm sure of it. We stand up and say something like LOVE IS COMING BACK BABY! You get what I'm saying?'

So this woman, this stranger with the sea swimmer body, frisky glint in the eye, the alco-hole in her face, wants to go into business with me. I still don't know what to think.

I'd said, 'I don't know if I can listen to people crying about being lonely.'

She'd said, 'But it's okay to listen to guys crying about not being man enough?'

'Fair point.'

'What motivates you, Denis? Helping people or making money?'

'Both.'

She went, 'But you do neither to any great extent, right?'

'Wrong.'

'I go where my instinct leads me. You know what I mean?'

I said, 'So did your instinct say to go into business with me after sniffing my hand?'

She said, 'I smelled a stuck guy, a guy treading water. I smelled no care, no quality. I smelled fake cologne and fake leather. The cuff of that fancy shirt of yours says if you paid more than a fiver for it you were had. I got a good look at that Rolex too, the one with a hand that does not sweep the way a Rolex hand should. And I bet if I got a good mechanic to look at that big dick vehicle of yours, I'd find it was maybe less desirable than you'd like people to think. You're faking it big time Denis, faking it until you make it. When do you think that will be? Hmm?'

I said nothing.

'So,' she said, 'yes is the answer. I smelled your palm and it left me thinking you could do with a break, that we could give each other a break. We can be a good team. What do you think? Wanna swim in some dirty water together?'

I said, 'I can't work you out.'

She said, 'I'm the same as you.'

'You think? How so?'

'Just the same.

'Example?'

'My husband's dead. That's one way.'

'I'm sorry to hear that.'

Eyes over-dramatically darting around the car park, she whispered, 'I killed him.'

Fifteen

Assert: The bigger test is not in handling adversity but in handling power.

A LONG tombstone of light on the sandy ground ahead. Kill the engine and exit. Strip off and into the water, sea level rising to the neck. Head under, a twist in the brine, a tight corkscrew to missile me out further and further and further.

Up for breath and the cars are crawling the far hills, electric parasites wriggling on the big banks around the city. I've come to look at everything from my dirty beauty spot, this waxy hangout. I've come to swim hard away and see if I make it back.

Upright now, torso gripped in the most treacherous hold and I'm floating, treading, bobbing. I'm out here to take custody of me, to once more take charge of saving myself. I've swum more than a mile out this time and I've to do it again if I want to live.

But here I am in the hardest place making my hard decisions, seeking to work it all out. Back there on the land, all those lucky people know everything already. They can find out anything in the world in a heartbeat. Everyone there knows they're worth it too because they're told it so many times. They deserve to have their faces praised and thoughts amplified, to be loved for showing their billion friends their colours because they're on an invisible promise to trade the same in return, to swap not give. Everyone there deserves only the best and everyone else is making sure they get it.

They share wisdom so generously there, from house to house, screen to screen, sofa to sofa. They love the axioms back there, all those wise ones who read astonishing sentiment and conclusions while taking a shit. They love words that formed in the greatest minds, words that changed lives, words that cracked through and captured as they went. They swap other people's wisdom around like pictures of dead celebrities now, hawking that stuff to each other in exchange for stuff hawked back. It's one big axiom sale, one big dump of achievement, of everything there ever was. There's a big real wisdom sale because fake everyone is fake ready for it because they've blurred their wrinkles and bugged-up their eyes and put a flag on their fake face. There's a big sale now everyone in the world has said *you couldn't make it up* or *let that sink in* or *I don't even know* or *I'll just leave this here* or *OMFG!* or *what could possibly go wrong?* No truth of the ages will escape being prostituted, will escape becoming a valueless and fleeting currency. No great truth, no great words will survive mass production to the point they become meaningless to people who already know everything without know-how, who love everything with no love to make. Fiz said it best when she said connection to everyone is connection to no one.

So when I write this book, I'll say something like 'Fuck the masses.' I'll say, 'Fuck society.' When I get stuck in, I'll say I'm antifragile now.

My shoulders hurt.

My damn head hurts.

I'm spitting here, this filmy stinking fish-killing shit's in my face, my mouth. I'm spitting and embarking on some kind of relationship with a drunk life coach who might be a killer who reads palms with her nose. I'm spitting and trying to track down Californian's finest because she's been talking to Fiz's family and

Did She See You?

Mim and it's all eating away at my finely balanced life like a virus.

When I hear myself think it like that it makes me want to stay in this shipping lane, to wait around and see how it flushes me out. It's so easy to just start breathing this salty piss, to let my brain unravel and slip on down into the arrant black. I'd never bother even thinking about this relentless shit again, never get back to Bet, never think of Dagny again, never have to even know how it all turns out. There's nothing above this water holding me here, nothing between me and a billion indifferent stars. Underneath, all I've got are these plain, pale, pistoning legs and flapping arms, a dozen muscles that don't give a damn if they are dead or alive in an hour.

Axiom for sale! You'll be smarter once you know it. It applies everywhere. It's a great truism. Fuck with it at your peril. You can take it off my hands for a smile, a wink.

Axiom for sale! Take it home for a like, for a damn retweet.

Axiom for sale! Got one here that inspired incredible things and you can have it for a misspelt comment, an emoji, a kiss, for being my friend.

Axiom for sale! It's on my smartphone right now. Read it quick as it flies out the fucking window.

I face the shore, ready to reach into the hard journey ahead, to throw open this wingspan and commit to terra firma. Legs are heavy. Flanks of meat, long pigs I've to drag now for a mile. And in among the quiet platinum tips of this black plain I see a figure, a noisemaking, moving shape. It's splashing, limbs whirling, swimming towards where I am. Another crazed bather, another refugee, its head tucked low, arms butterfly-style, closing in. Is this real?

I wipe at my face now, still marching, stamping the water. I rub my eyes and look again and it's there, this powerful mover winning over the water. I feel I should get out of the way, that I'll need to let this sea pilot pass. Aimed right at me, fifty feet now. This is one freaky thing to see out here.

And it stops, tilts from horizontal to vertical. It drops its legs, starts treading just like me, hanging here just like me. It gasps, rubs its unclear face just the way I just did. It's breathing seriously heavily, is seriously exhausted. I can't tell gender, size, shape. Just a ghoulish blob in the black. It breathes in deeper, sucking in that stink, drawing as much as it can now into its lungs, readying to do something.

I go to call, and I've got nothing more than a sharp sigh, an exit of hot breath. I'm so exhausted, a mile to go to save my life. I'm here too long, arms failing now, legs numb. I go to call again and nothing comes. And the figure slips down and vanishes into the ink.

My brain stopping, starting, filling with alarm and questions. It urges me to get to the shore, and to dive down, to do two things at once but both cannot be done.

I barely make it back, numb legs scraping on the seabed. I'm retching, fainting, dragging myself from the little waves. I couldn't have gone any further and survived.

I'm catching my breath, washed up in the dark and there's a couple, an older man and wife walking the shore at secluded Quarrel Bay. I lie here, hoping they don't see me or come to save me, hoping they leave me alone with my burning limbs, my tiny balls, my diesel skin, my turmoiled mind. They have this mini-

Did She See You?

Schnauzer, its beard giving it an ethereal, wizardy look. I'm passing out as it spots me, strains on its lead, barks. I'm naked, overwhelmed by nature, as undone a person as you could find in a city.

'Evening,' your man says, continuing to walk on by.

'Hi.'

I'm wondering if someone is dead out there, if a body will wash up on the shore tonight. I want to sleep, to just let go. Eyes closed and I think about the dead dummy with the torn neck on the sofa.

I wake up shivering. I wake up like something respawned, a loser with a second chance.

I stand, wind in my ears, walk shivering to the Disco. I climb in to get dressed. It's 5AM and I'm thinking again of Dagny now, of how I can again try to reach her, ask her how she dared go see Fiz's family, how she dared bluff her way in to see Mim. I can't believe it and completely believe it at the same time.

I get the coat on, start the engine, crank up the heat. I call her for the seventh time since yesterday. Still no answer.

'Shit.'

As I go to drive off, I scan along the shore, out into the water, just to see what I can see, but there's nothing to catch the eye. I put on the lights, buckle up, move.

At home and I'm sensing that dead dummy looking at me with no eyes. I look at that thing, at the hole in its neck and feel like killing it again, like doing the crazy blade attack on it once more if only I had the strength. Is there any satisfaction to be had from that? Would it get me any peace of mind? The shape of that thing, like it almost has a mouth, almost a curve where its lips could be.

My phone dings and I'm looking down and I swear I hear that dummy speak. I am freaking myself out with the idea that it just used a mouth it doesn't have to say something it can't. I've got a text from Dagny and I look back up at the glossy cream skin on that thing because a little crazy part of me is sure it just whispered, *'Did she see you?'*

Dagny's text goes, 'What?'
'Are you still here?'
'Why?'
'Did you go and see Mim?'
'Why?'
'Did you?'
'Yes.'
'What the fuck?'
'Jeez. Don't get up so early if you're not a morning person.'
'She is damaged, you sanctimonious moron. All over the place when I saw her last, thanks to you.'
'She was fine with me.'
'Fine? Nice word for it.'
'For what?'
'For her madness,' I write. 'Stop lying. She and I were building and you waded in saying whatever bullshit you said to her. Meet me.'
'Meet you? Why? And she's not mad. She's nice.'
'Then you're mad too.'
'Saw no signs of madness, Denis. Locked up to make things easy for you and the state. That's it. She needs to get out of there.'
'You don't know the first thing about her.'

Did She See You?

'FYI, yes I do. She was lucid. Answered my questions. Denies killing her mother, by the way. She said to ask you, *'Did she see you?'*

Sixteen

Assert: I just go out there and get it.

FIZ would never have aborted. That was murder to her, the intentional killing of a family member. The ugliness of the conception had no bearing on it. It came up in school, in teenage life, and she never wavered. She was from deep within a family, from inside a tradition where that option remained obscene, cruel and always avoidable. She would have said there was no sin of the father great enough to warrant such a punishment for the child.

She had a grandmother who pledged to support her all the way. Old Freda told her that the man who attacked her was lucky that her father was dead, that he would have killed him. Fiz never did say his name.

She did not go to the police. She blamed herself for all of it, was ever resolute that she was responsible for all that emerged from her own behaviour. She used the situation as a spur to clean herself up - her mind, her body, her bloodstream. I look back at all of that, her immense decision to take on that child, and I know she was wrong. The child who gave the mother reason to rebuild herself went on to take the mother's life.

She came to me at fourteen weeks, at her weakest and her most vulnerable and I couldn't let her go. Love did what love does and I took her as my wife. I will never regret it.

'No, there have been no visits since,' Shadi says.
'Okay. Where's Dr Harriet? She's not responding to me.'

Did She See You?

He nods, says, 'Time off. She'll be back soon.'
'Holidays?'
'Just tired.'
'Who's her replacement?'
'Dr Cooper. But his patient number has just increased. He might not be able to spend as much time with Miriam as Harriet does. It might affect your arrangements.'

He looks away now, down to his papers. He wants me to leave him alone.

I glance to the end of the room. She's rocking uselessly side to side, back and forwards, a busted metronome that will never stop.

Shadi goes, 'Did she see you -'

It swirls fast in my head, makes me blink and I turn to him, snap, 'What?'

'Did Dr Harriet see you the last time? I think she was planning to explain to you about Dr Cooper. Perhaps you have forgotten?'

'No. Forgotten? No. The last time I was here I spoke with you. You said someone had been to see Mim.'

'Oh yes,' he says.

'I want more on that, Shadi. On the visitor. How did she arrange that? I mean, can anyone just walk in and see her?'

'Any person can make a request. Primarily it is the decision of the patient but in some cases, like with Miriam, it is also considered by her doctor.'

'Who was it?'

'You know I can't say. Dr Harriet can advise...'

'How did it go, that meeting? How was Miriam's mood?'

'I can only say that I think she just talked as she always does.'

'What about?'

'I can't say, of course. I don't know.'

'Has she been okay since?'

'There is no change.'

I sit down to face her once more and feel tired, hungry, low. She tenses and my whole body tenses in response. The stupid joust lies ahead and I can't bear the thought today. Just looking at her sun-scraped face and seared eyes is draining me, emptying me out. Her life is better than mine right now. She can do and say whatever she wants, eat and sleep and talk and walk and never do anything wrong again. Her cage is her comfort.

Serious tone, I go, 'Mim?'

'...*Margaret Rutherford and beans dis da way and in time for eleven fivers centrally dear heart...*'

Grumpy, annoyed, I go, 'Mim.'

'...*spandex for Gary FWIW renal failure is more common now coming like a ghost town 60 today...*'

'Mim. I want you to listen to me.'

'...*sparkles when it is taken blank and blind cunty balls...*'

'Mim,' I whisper, 'I know you.'

'...*lance from root off deadhead to another sticker on an ashes room we strongly believe can yes mate...*'

'Mim?'

'...*cast off like shit you think Kim K good interaction Jim Wells hole monopoly up yer kilt cider...*'

'Miriam,' I whisper, 'I have a what if.'

'...*advertising operations coordinator no chips...*'

Maybe she doesn't have to think about it anymore. Maybe her mind has hardwired the pattern. A mountain

Did She See You?

of miscellaneous words collected and all she does is flick them off, roll them down the hill, slide out the lies with the greatest of ease. Maybe it's easier to do this thing than not do it.

Could it be this woman, this girl, this deep trench of a kid, is making herself madder? It can't be easy for her to hold onto what's left of what works in that brain, not while doing this around the clock. So have I got this wrong? Do I, in the end, have no hope of finding the girl among the words? Am I losing her to this invention? Is her strategy so good, so flawless that she's made herself become her idea?

'...Cujo was among them access into the wider blank fanny on it get childhood's over I saw no signs of madness watch to the end...'

I say, 'What did you think of Dagny O'Reilly?'

'...your favourite colour would be your favourite get apples the stuff that covers we all stare at our shit rising up back on it...'

'Did you talk to her? She says you did.'

'...nobody on the paradise four four five nine when the call came get chips and fuck sake nothing...'

I go, 'She's famous, she says. Probably told you.'

'...five five in the entertainment industry new boundaries says McHugh September is awareness nah bollocks you...'

'A YouTuber.'

'...on the court is her quiet time click or call insurance choices 80p collateral gets messy get this done x send nudes racing tennis...'

'She wants to film our story. She wants me to tell her all about you, about what you did, and I don't want to.'

Jason Johnson

'...big city attitude wild horses from Cavan outsourced personality roulette 800 years...'

I tell her I saw a swimmer hold their breath and drop down into the place that would kill them. I tell her I'm finding direction in Bet, that she's badass and maverick and reminds me of Fiz and is offering me some kind of plan I couldn't even consider up to now.

And Mim mumbles on like background music and I say, 'I never felt like your real dad. Your real dad is a rapist, right? You know that, don't you? Did your mother tell you? I hated him before I met you so maybe that's one reason we never made it, never worked as a family. Maybe that's why you never loved me, because I never loved you like I would a real daughter, not really. I tried. Maybe you did too. But it was all so noisy, so claustrophobic. Your condition was just...'

'...phone a cab try to keep a lid on it Paul and the agreements wah wahs benefits and protections 70p in the sand Boris round axiom retweet and round collar felt...'

'...but I know you loved your mum. I know you loved her non-stop, in your own way. And I did too. That's why this is so important, this thing I do, this question. I have to know Mim. I wish you knew how much I needed to know. It's like everything hangs on that moment. It's like a nail I got caught on and can't get free. Do you understand? I have to know what she saw, Mim. When she was in front of that mirror, as she was turning towards you...'

'...necessary is wrong unplug it ffs hot tubs are for perverts buy a side of it assume you're already friends when first meeting worms weary day...'

'...I have to know if her eyes were up at that point, if she was already looking at you; if she saw what was

Did She See You?

happening as she turned. I go back to that moment again and again and again and I can't breakaway I have to know, yes or no, if she knew who killed her...'

'...digital solution is perfecto don't you dare fart lol...'

I go, 'Dagny says you asked her to ask me the same question. I can't believe her. I know you've no reason to do that. But I also don't understand how she could know what it is I ask you. Did it come up when you met? Did it Mim? Did you tell Dagny I ask *Did she see you?*'

'...remedy volatile for bastard regular Ormeau footwear oh lordy hodl hodl sheer weight 2095...'

And, Christ, there's a tear in my eye. I wipe it fast. I blink fast. I change frame and rework and take nothing personally.

I am a high value alpha male and this is where I am being a high value alpha male nothing can stop me being a high value alpha male.

I sit up straight, hard outthink this emotion. I clear my throat and stab my shiny eyes now into her marred face.

'What did Dagny say, Mim?'

'...character is the best way smart new socks look pure here...'

'Should I go and meet her again, find out? She's ignoring my calls, might have left the country for all I know. But I need to know what you said. I mean, are we about to pop up on the internet? You, me, your mum? Our family story? That would kill me Mim, it would kill me. Don't you kill me that way.'

And I can hear it, see it. I can feel her picking up the pace, lifting the volume, responding to this pressure of mine.

'...eggs in your tea put it into second gear get wine and nuts...'

'Miriam. Listen.'

'...Sooky needs his brekky comes across as very cynical don't suggest hormones morning David...'

I whisper, 'Miriam. What did you say about that night?'

'...citizenship ceremony IGZ is not a meme don't be there sales is a different thing it's true and there's no denying...'

Faster, louder.

'...goes back deeper if I take that subway will do mustard mostly safe recently shimmering light in car park...'

'Hey, you.'

'...somebody else where they need to start ring me babes grey car prob Nissan shame is not where it remembers central walks with a stick...'

Slamming those words together.

'Miriam?'

'...in the tower and up a tree doorbell black is the colour persist did she see Kiera...'

'Did she ask about that moment? You remember that moment? The living room? The gun in your hand?'

'...cranky enough in the mornings whether he has sought a line in the upcoming budget run Deacon and 17 run point out smoke cannister to indicate...'

'When your mum turned towards you. You remember? The last time you saw her?'

'...person so cute and describing the dancing knows your friend so coffee from 9.30AM you persist...'

'The last time you saw her. The very last second you saw her.'

Did She See You?

'...plus point in my world communications manager and his horse spectacles aunt was in Benidorm run...'

'Let's find out, will we Mim?'

'...send it flying going back now it's 1999...'

'Did she see you?'

'...rascal choppy in CBI panic is dancing with me wild boys authorised by increments run love cards...'

She's a train in all its motion now, shooting along, full speed.

I go, 'We can end this, end these meetings. If you tell me. It's all I need to know. I'd do anything in return. If you asked. Anything.'

'...five seven oh five college have you seen this bringing on the heart in west end Malone don't buy the persist buns in pans...'

'Did she see you?'

'...sensible weed stock in fences beyond gmail dot com review table ghost town on the ceiling so you...'

'Did she see you?'

'...brace charm in the bursting rally burning like first out of hell up your nose...'

'It'd be the last time you'd hear me ask it, the last ever time.'

'...lisp within context of drama mind how you go...'

'Just once more...'

'...bit that fits in space fortnight blanket don't fret awkward men society run run...'

'...did she see you?'

'...'

She stops. The whole place falls silent.

My heart freezes. My lungs. My blood skids to a halt. I feel everyone turning, looking at this place of massive quiet.

All eyes on us. My eyes on her. It's the longest, biggest nothing. One second. Two seconds.

Then the mouth moves, tremors, murmurs, and it all bubbles up again, climbs in her throat and out her mouth again. And back to the babble of those nosy visitors, the crazy clients, the skew-whiff patients, the criminally insane and their sidekicks.

She goes, so quiet now, '...*there there there there there there there there there goes with the frisbee give Alan a rest Sky News BBC News GB News relative you look amazing shapes on offer...*'

So low, 'Did she see you?'

'...*put it into the mine can Keith even read where is the radio...*'

'Did she see you?'

'...*Salt Lake City and further poor heart aches god is great juniper berries placing the forceps...*'

'Mim.'

'...*messy peaches run and other assorted FTP delights...*'

'Did she see you?'

'...*China is a part of the empire...*'

'Did she see you?'

'...*like placing wheels under the mice...*'

'Come on.'

'...*however it might be if there was no market bell end persist...*'

'Tell me.'

'...*accentuate the journey of atoms oh seven three three eight...*'

'Did she see you?'

'...*Noirmoutier and an intermission locked away bonfires like jenga run...*'

'Did she see you?'

Did She See You?

'...as a secure in one or two lots gender-based pain in pain out did it on Weds...'

'Did she see you?'

'...preparations dashing the revolutionary end Yes straddling the shape of the roller people buy people and Milewater Road...'

It's selfish, coming here. It's an underhand act wrapped up as virtue. But we'll be done one day and she'll be better without me. She'll find a way to stop. She'll realise she no longer needs this vast shield.

This girl here used to do so much more, used to move non-stop, machine-gun her energy all over the place. She used to jump up and down like a Pogo stick, used to yell at the sky like some spellbound maniac. One time I found her under the stairs playing something on her phone. She turned the screen, showed me a little film she made of her kicking the fence over and over and over and over and over. Her foot was bare, its toes all busted and broken. She kept kicking it, kicking and kicking. Toes, foot, all bent out of shape. Bones exposed, split, shattered, blood on the wood. No sign of pain, just joy at the extremity of the sensation. She was editing the video, making a little story, a little pocketbook tale of her day for herself, bleeding and telling a story.

I said, 'I'll get some water and bandages, call one of the net doctors. Don't let your mum see that video, okay?'

And she didn't answer, never answered. Her whole life was just posed question after question and I've never been able to resolve any of it.

But today, just now, we had a breakthrough, didn't we? Did we? Did something happen? Did we move forward?

I look at her now, tune back in, watch a hand flick up, tuck no hair behind her little left ear. I put my left hand on the desk, tap the fingers, know she can see it.

'... buying the new curtains do it unwinding at the spa do it reveals the success of the tactic concurrent activity is a principle of war...'

'What can I do for you, Mim.'

'...end of the line cannot know where you are going without a map...'

'What can I do for you?'

'...out out in the blaze where rap shapes shit and calm...'

'Is there something I can do for you?'

'...out out where weeks and tunes complete charity flashpoint here in the beaks two grams mate run run...'

'Be as clear as you can, Mim. Try to find the words. Try to grab them from your mind as they pass. Try to find the words you need. Say the words that might work as an answer? Can you find some? Can you find any words to answer when I ask if there's something I can do for you?'

'...bailey street and negative Sam's got it burnish shame with the pot see you on a redacted bible sharing a shadow run if arsonist of lives...'

'Can you grab a word? Anything that works? Just try it.'

'...lustre space and slow the roll manners wings and salad anti-semite bingo out and out did she go out and out persist yes what crisis...'

'Keep trying, Mim. You can do it. Use the words you can hear. Grab one. Just grab one. Let the obstacle become the way? Do you understand? Take control of what's in front of you, Mim. Let the obstacle become the way, okay?'

Did She See You?

'...messing perfection in the weak point stick dick in crazy see you down and out run with the king...'

'Just picture the word you need and it'll be there, okay? Just try it, okay?'

'...out out out out out...'

My heart ramps up a gear, I go, 'You selected that word? Out? You want out? Is that what you're saying to me?'

'...out out out out...'

'You want out?'

She goes, '...out out out get out get out get out get out get out...'

Jason Johnson

Seventeen

Assert: A lack of action is a lack of courage.

FREDA doesn't walk at all, says she hasn't walked a step in six months. I'm wheeling her to the exit and she goes, 'The legs are just a burden now. Deadweight.'
I say, 'You don't need the use of them where you're going.'
Bet has done the old lady's hair, applied a bright red lipstick, bought her a nice frock, helped put it on. The camera's rolling as we move out into the sunlight. The glare is too strong for small Freda's cloudy eyes. Bet swiftly slides my big mirrors onto her face.
I lean down, put my lips to Freda's ear, say, 'Fiz would've loved this,' and she gives a little hum, slowly raises a hand to the journalist watching her every move.
We lift Freda into the Disco, Bet and I. We drive off and the camera cuts, gets packed away for the next location.
The old Spitfire gleams as we pull up, all glory and sparkle in the low sun. Freda purses her thin lips at first sight. The recognition's clear, comforting. I look in the mirror at Bet, holding the old lady's powerless hand, and we smile a good smile.
Bomber Joe's already in the cockpit, pre-hoisted in by the overhead crane. He wears a leather helmet, goggles on the forehead. His old RAF outfit, last worn for a funeral a decade ago, has rarely looked as grand. Bomber Joe's never flown a Spitfire, but he knows more about them than anyone you know. Most importantly, he knows how to sit in an icon, how to revere one, how to behave in its presence. And so does Freda. She spent

Did She See You?

twenty years painting them onto plates, canvas and walls and anywhere else she was commissioned to do so.

Camera rolling again and Bomber Joe raises a gloved hand as we lift Freda into the harness. As the winch turns, he pats the side of the plane, a painted heart under his hand.

'Come on in, girl,' he calls as Freda's hoisted skywards.

The plane's private owner, on a ladder against the cockpit, helps disconnect the harness, strap her into this terrier of bygone skies, this proven heart breaker, life stopper. I climb the ladder on the other side, hold the old lady's hand as she's packed into the seat, check she's okay.

Freda is loud, shouting now like the engine's already running. She goes, 'Is Miriam here?'

I say, 'No. Miriam's not here today, Freda.'

'Is Miriam having a go in the Spitfire?'

'No. Is that okay?'

'Yes,' she says, 'I'm glad.'

'I understand,' I say.

'She killed my daughter.'

'She killed your granddaughter.'

'That was bad.'

'I know, Freda. Fiz was my wife.'

'What?'

'Fiz was my wife. Remember?'

'Oh yes,' she goes, laughs, 'the tanned fella. You never impressed the family.'

'I know,' I say, 'but I don't give a fuck.'

Freda in the shades laughs more and I lean forward, kiss her forehead.

The owner, opposite me, dips out of sight and Bet arrives at the top of the ladder, the old plane and its two hundred years of people on board. Bet looks priceless today, looks better every time I see her. There she is now, shining, sober, hydrated, happy, all self-possession and eyes on me as she hands Freda a rose.

I say, 'Have you seen who's flying the plane, Freda?'

She goes, 'I hope it's not me.'

Bomber Joe, an old friend from old air shows, can barely turn, but does his best, shows the side of his goggled face to the half-blind woman in mirror sunglasses.

'Freda, my darling,' he says, 'how nice to see you again.'

'Ack, hello Bomber. Sure I seen you last week. Bus not good enough for you anymore?'

'Haha! How're you keeping, my love? Still sweet sixteen?'

'Oh yes,' she goes, 'and fit as a trout.'

Bomber Joe can't fly it, wouldn't be allowed even if he could. But, after a lot of negotiation, he's allowed to take the fighter for a spin around the airfield. It amounts to the same thing for Freda. She smiles as the engine starts. The owner turns to me, ashen faced, says nothing.

'They'll be fine,' I say.

'It's my plane I'm worried about,' he says.

'It's been through worse.'

Chocks away, they trundle off, a buzzing metal Bluebottle on its predetermined lap for the next fifteen minutes. With them in the background, we do the interview. We stand close and say we loved matchmaking these two, that we find people who want love, that we help them make it. We say we have a serious proposition for the single, for the unloved, for the weird, the sexless, the empty, the undone, the mad, for those who can't make romantic ends meet, of any age, any gender, any declaration.

I go, 'Those two lovebirds there in the Spitfire are on their third date now and we're pretty sure there will be a fourth.'

Bet goes, 'We're an agency of our times. People are more connected than ever, but many of them will know what I mean when I say that a remote connection keeps connection remote, that it increases disconnection. We have our doubts about the swipe and wipe process as means of finding love. So we're saying come to us. As coaches, we help people love and relaunch themselves and now we're moving up from that. The truth, if you read the runes, is that romance, real connection, is coming back because the need is greater than ever.'

I go, 'That's right. I mean, it's become almost normal to just lie about life, about happiness. All that shiny stuff online isn't always true. Our agency is about empowering anyone who knocks our door, about getting a genuine connection for them, about propelling them towards real intimacy and away from screens.'

We've set up a singles' night called Disconnect, where people ditch their phones, sit in a Chatham House Rules circle and speak about love, romance, the tingles, about what they want in their connection when they're at their most disarmingly unbrushed honest.

We've laid on a month of free coaching for singles, couples, triples, whatever, who want to build more love. We want people to raise their sights, fire up their engines and look our way. We're not offering tips, we're giving solutions. We're not boosting your love life, we're making sure you love life.

Says Bet, 'Remember, romance is coming back.'

We look over at the plane, at the cameraman crouching low to get upshots of the pair of them, both backgrounded by a rich blue sky and long wispy clouds like fantastic ghosts of the past.

The reporter asks, 'So are you two a couple, or should I not ask that?'

And we turn back to him because we knew this was coming. We knew it this morning and we laughed together after we told him he might want to ask. Bet and I had started this day making love in her bed, laughing as the tension mounted, turning serious and determined as nerve endings rang. We made love and left, running late for our appointment with the centenarian.

I look at Bet, still all newly charming from that bond, and my arm goes easily around her waist and I don't know if I'm falling in love but I love it. I pull her tight, kiss her cheek and she goes conveniently jelly, tilts her head forward like she's blushing.

I say, 'We just got engaged. This morning.'

The nurse claps. A doctor on standby claps. The camera falls on them as the nurse puts a hand to her chest and sighs.

The deep chopping of the plane carries on, the old warrior motoring along the runway, going nowhere, grounded forever, its pilot on his last hurrah, his ancient passenger fast asleep.

Eighteen

Assert: My life is brilliant and getting better.

DR HARRIET is confused, wants to know where I'm coming from with all this.

'I don't understand,' she goes.

I say, 'Mim wants out. Okay? Just for a few hours. It'd be good for her, right? I mean, I know this kind of thing does happen and I'm assuming you can start that process.'

'What are you saying to me, Denis? I mean, there's only so much we can do and I think we've been...'

'Look, I appreciate...'

She goes, 'The programme she is on is clear about where she can go and with who. But you know all that. Or maybe you don't? Do you understand what you're talking about here?'

'What I mean...'

'I know what you mean but I don't understand why I have to go through all this again.'

'Again?'

'Yes, again. I get the impression you don't always take on board what I say. I respect your dedication to Miriam, I really do. I respect the consistency of your visits. It's incredibly valuable. But I think you just switch off when you and I talk. Is that unfair?'

I shake my head, stand up, walk to the office door, planning only to walk back this way. I take a quick breath, hold the phone closer, speak a little quieter, a little more determined. I say, 'We have our wires crossed.'

She says, 'You have your wires crossed if you don't mind me saying. But look – I know things might have been uncomfortable and confusing lately. I have to tell you Shadi has told me he advised you that someone had visited Mim.'

'And I know very well who that was.'

'I am absolutely certain he did not give you a name.'

'He didn't need to. Her visitor was one Dagny O'Reilly. Correct?'

'I'm sorry?'

'Dagny O'Reilly.'

'Are you asking me if Miriam's visitor was called Dagny O'Reilly?'

'I'm telling you I know Miriam's visitor was Dagny O'Reilly, the American YouTuber.'

'Just to be clear, Mr Bic, I don't know anything about an American YouTuber visiting New Ready House.'

I go, 'Why would you? Why would Dagny have told you the truth?'

She says, 'I'm happy to advise you who the visitor was. I had decided to do so before this phone call. And I can assure you the visitor was not called Dagny O'Reilly.'

'Who was the visitor?'

'Her father.'

'Whose father?'

'Mim's father.'

I planned to begin the battle to get Mim out into the world for half a day. It had been to convince Harriet to consider that Mim needed a road, a river, a mountain, a park, a space to give her mind a shove. But everything's just changed.

Did She See You?

    Once again, I go, 'Her father?'
    'Yes.'
    'The fucking rapist?'
    'I'm sorry?'
    'Her father, her biological father? The guy who raped her mother and played no part in Mim's upbringing. That guy? That guy!?'
    'Okay. That's not... I wasn't aware of that.'
    'Holy shit, Harriet.'
    I am all kinds of outrage.

    I can't sleep. A day since that call and it's become a rational decision to go see her cousin, Raymond the Rapist. This will not be an angry thing, not a journey driven by hatred. I've done my hating, I've told myself. I've hated him enough to kill him, to kill me. But now it has become entirely reasonable for me to enquire why he visited Mim and why now? I want to know what his game is, what his interest is in the daughter of the relative he raped.
    I'm on the Lower Newtownards Road looking into long Templemore Avenue. My back's against a red, raging fist, a balled assertion of status among a chain of painted walls. The images, numbers and symbols, combine like code, a thumbprint advising of provenance, confirming identity. They're a line in the sand, a scowling, loaded allegiance barrier telling you where you are and who you are with.
    At a mid-terrace house a few feet from a church, it looks as if anyone in there is dead. Curtains are closed on unwashed windows, weeds are snaking along the front step, a busted rainspout is sputtering like some failed exhaust system. Raymond's house has the air of a place of function, no-frills, no love. Thinking back, it

always was. His was always a party house and now, after the crazy years have fallen away, that brightness has dimmed deep.

I knock, knuckles sharp. The door sounds hollow, a probable cheap replacement of a smashed-in predecessor. I knock again, three more times. My hand feels hard, ready to knock more. I feel brazen, crude, fully able to punch a man who needs a punch, able to deck a man who has rocked a boat he should not have rocked. So I reframe, douse the emotion, take nothing personally. I explain inside how the animal brain is crossing over and it wants to drag me into a battle that will not serve me in the end.

And still no sound from inside. I look around. The night's sinking beyond twilight, the tired amber of the streetlights arriving. I might not come here again if he's not here now.

I step back, look up. Those dark old curtains are thick and closed and without comment. I'm thinking about TV licence people, about welfare fiddles, about petty crime and hard drink and drugs. That's all this house is now. There was a time when the front door was flung open and music charged into the street. Now it's a house that just wants to be invisible.

I knock again, more hard raps. Neighbours will be watching, thinking I'm a bailiff, a cop, a man here to extract some cash or revenge from a hopeless addict who made a mess of lives around him.

A clunk from inside. A lock or key. Something has been engaged, something metal. The door opens. There's no light inside either, the darkest house on the street.

I breathe, straighten my back, feel my heart squeeze and push inside me. My shoulders lift and there's a stink of old booze and ash, of the end of the fun.

I am higher value than any of this because I am a high value alpha male and I will find out what I need to know here.

The woman's putting her glasses on, straightening the thick frames with a skinny-wristed left hand. She pulls the door to reveal all her face, but only just. Even in the darkness she looks unwell, has stains on her grubby T-shirt, looks as if she's just been sick. The untended face is gaunt, its character evicted by toxins, lips pale, hair a dried mess of dye and grey. Her nose, rich with blackheads, crunches as she looks at my hair.

'Looking for Raymond.' My tone's low, lower than I expected. It's a growl.

She shakes her head.

'You police?'

I don't react.

'Is he here?'

She shakes her head again, her eyes squinting as she tries to work out my face.

I go, 'Are you... Joan?'

She's looking and searching for some clue to cue up a response. But nothing.

I say, 'You're Joan, aren't you? Raymond's wife?'

She does it again, searching my face.

I say, 'I'm Denis. We met before. Many times. Old friend of Raymond's. Does he still live here?'

She's got nothing. No recognition, no memory. But it's enough to oil the wheels. She pulls the door open further, steps back a little, goes, 'Aye. Denis. I remember you. He's upstairs.'

I don't believe she remembers.

I go, 'Okay.'

She goes, eyeing me closer, smiling now, 'Back again for more, eh?'

I shake my head. She remembers something of parties that should never have happened. I say, 'No, Joan. No more.'

Her nose drops back, the smile goes away. She tilts her head into the house.

I pause. But there's nothing to think about here, is there? About them, about me? I'm not going to take any shit, not at this place. The useless freak and his rotting wife have ended up old and weak before their time and, I tell myself, that's revenge enough.

I step in and summon courage before taking a breath. I'm thinking of bile, of skidmarks, of rats, of lice. She closes the door. There's a single light on, a lamp, in the living room to the right. A television's running, volume low, shapes flickering in the hall. She nods upwards and I can tell she's unwell. She could be his mother, his grandmother, but she can't be more than forty.

'Raymond,' she says, the ingredients for an upcoming chesty cough in her mouth now, 'party time.'

She laughs as she turns. She's going back to the living room and expecting me to go upstairs. Raymond's saying nothing.

'Is he in bed?' I say.

'No he's in Disneyland,' she says, her back to me.

I don't touch the banister as I take the first step, yet my hands are out of my pockets, fists itching to clench. Beating the shit out of someone would not be the worst crime committed in this grim place, but I'm taking nothing personally to get this done, to make sure his visit doesn't happen again.

Did She See You?

At the top and I call, 'Joan? No lights up here?'

She reaches back into the hall, to a wall switch, flicks it. Nothing.

'It's on now,' she says and goes back into the living room, chuckling again.

I go, a shade angry, 'I should have brought a bulb, you waster.' I know she'll have heard it and know she'll not give a damn.

The carpet's thick. I can tell it's filthy, hard, sticky, even through my shoes. Yellow from a streetlight is making it through a window, low-lighting the corridor.

'Raymond,' I say, clear and firm.

The master bedroom door's open, no one visible on the unmade bed. The other, the box room above the front door, is closed. There's a couple of old shoes on the floor where I stand, a dark coat half hanging over the rail.

I hate this house.

I knock on the little room.

'Raymond?'

And nothing. But I've come this far.

A hand on the doorknob, a twist. Pitch black inside. The smell of life being unlived, of unchallenged decay, of a bed pissed a dozen times, of the complete absence of love. And I whisper it now, as I try to make out what I can see on the little single bed.

I go, 'Raymond? It's Denis.'

To the man lying down below where I stand, I say, 'Raymond?'

I reach for a switch, flick it. And again nothing. I pull out my phone, swipe upwards, select the little torch. It beams out, spotlights a plate at my feet, a couple of hard chips, a hard blob of red sauce, a couple of mouse droppings. There's a lighter. Some pants. A hammer. A foot out of the end of the bed. Long, hard nails on long, hairy toes. Stained pink duvet like something a hated dog would sleep on. I imagine crusty cum marks and an army of ravenous bedbugs.

There's something over his face, over his head. It's neat, pulled on carefully, pulled over tight like a too-big Covid mask. I can see the lump of his nose, the troughs of his eyes. It's embracing him from chin to forehead, like something for him to breathe through. Or something for him to not breathe through. Because Raymond is not breathing. If I was to hazard a guess, Raymond's dead.

'Raymond?'

My hand, my fingers, hovering over the material, ready to pick it off, to reveal for the first time in eighteen years the face of the man who raped my wife. I never wanted to see him since that night, yet I've wanted to see him on this day. And now...

No. I need to call an ambulance, call the cops. Has he just put this thing on his face and died? Am I sure he's dead? From what? I need to get out of here.

I look into the grimy, grim corridor, at the patch of pale light made dirty as it rests on the rotten carpet. My nose is telling me I'm smelling recent death, a fresh end inside this hellish hovel just a wall away from normality.

And screw him, this bastard's death is no loss. I can lose nothing by knowing for sure. I flick the light back to his head, onto the white material, a brownish stain visible on one edge of it now. My fingers go to pick it from his face. It's not a cloth. It's a hat, a white baseball hat, the peak pulled back over the top of his head, pointing down into the pillow. I see a little insignia on its side now, it reads, 'LA Dodgers'.

Did She See You?

'Christ,' I say.

I'm looking at Fiz's hat, Fiz's baseball cap. The cap from my office. The cap I've never removed from my office. How has he got this? How is this now over her rapist's dead face?

The heart, my heart, tempo rising, squeezing firmer, releasing faster, panic mode. Blood charging madly through limbs as if seeking a way out. Flight, fight, freeze. Anxiety rocketing. Make a decision. Flight, fight, freeze.

'Hey,' I call, my voice higher, turning to the door as if the freak downstairs is going to be of any help to anyone.

'Hey,' I say it louder, 'Joan!'

And nothing. I take a step towards the door, to call it into the house, to call for that half-alive woman to come and help me cope. But now I hold my tongue.

I step back. I don't think about it. My fingers are on the peak now, the peak of my wife's cap, pulling it upwards, lifting what's been mine off this face.

'Christ,' I say again.

Eyes like mean, cold, blackened gun barrels. A hole in the side of the head, an inch-wide crater deep into his mind, surrounded by bruising. The light shows brain matter in the skull, reveals spongy crumbs of it dotted inside the rim of the obscene gap. He looks like no one now that he has this gape in his skull. He looks like it didn't matter. He looks like anyone, like no one. He smells like chicken, like copper, like mud and shit. My hand grips the cap, rolls it up. Whatever happens, it's not staying here.

Heart steadier now, high value courage now, I kill the light, step away, step out of this, away from this. Out of the room, almost tripping over a shoe on the corridor, pacing back to the top of the stairs. A noise now. A creak, maybe a door moving. There's movement from the room, from the double room, its door fully ajar. But how? There's no one there. It's just that something's fallen, something's slipped or tumbled. That's all.

Foot on the top step, ready to go, to quit this hole and now another noise. A sigh. A breath out, a breath in. From the room I didn't enter. I can barely look up. Too dark. Can't see anything. Fumble to get the phone's light back on but I don't want to, don't want to see whatever this is.

But it's happening.

I am an alpha fucking male fuck you I am a fearless alpha male I will not run from you fuck you I am high value.

Someone's breathing in, breathing out.

And a little voice, quiet, urgent, goes, 'Denis?'

I'm looking over and someone's standing there, a simple silhouette with every advantage over me.

I am a...

It goes, 'Denis?'

'Christ,' I go, 'Christ.' Stunned.

She goes, 'Did you not see me?'

Dagny lifts her phone, triggers her light, aims its beam at my face in this awful minute and its awful place.

'Talk to me,' she goes, still so quiet, still in a whisper.

I put a hand up to block the stinging glare. I can barely find language, but it comes, it goes, 'What the fuck?'

My heart's thumping hard as hell, banging, ears like they're underwater. I'm urging myself to get out of

Did She See You?

here. Heart and head say the decision has been made and my legs are moving, taking me down.

At the bottom, Joan calls, 'Did you see him?'

I go, 'I...', and I don't know. I can't understand. I just want out.

Joan calls, 'Did he see you?'

I go, 'You're fuc...'

And Joan chuckles, a noise that's about to become a brutal, dirty cough, a messy spit. I look up and Dagny's there with her unwanted star throwing its rays, spotlighting me from the top of the stairs. She turns the light to herself as I'm stopped, staring, stuck on her image. And she shows me it's really her, her smallness and fatness and split hair dyed bright stupid pink, two sheens off rigid, round eyes. A glittering T-shirt, big white-rimmed glasses. She's holding the phone like she's some kind of angel, some kind of amazement from above. The rich Californian, the YouTube star at the top of those stairs on this street as my heart drums to her show.

She calls, louder now, in way too friendly a voice, 'Hey Denis, wait up.'

Joan's coughing, hacking and spitting away in the living room. I'm thinking she could die now, that I could die now. I'm thinking I could drop dead right here on the floor, heart beaten to death, brain worked down to nothing as Joan falls off the sofa, choked on sticky gob. I'm thinking how Dagny would film it all.

I'm thinking of everything I've learned, and I can't think of a thing to say. Words of courage, fortitude, resilience, change, action – they've all just stopped moving in my mind. I turn the snib, pull the door. The half-dead light from the street leans in, the unloved, indifferent, functional urban evening. No one around, no signs of life but for a low glow from inside a car further along the street. A couple of people parked up and sitting doing nothing, heads bowed, staring at screens. They don't see me as I take a breath, pull the door closed, nice and gentle, dip my head, walk away, my dead wife's hat screwed up tight in a hand.

Nineteen

Assert: Every attitude is a choice.

    I DON'T want sleep. I don't want rest or dreams or stillness, don't want to be refreshed. I need something else. I need the reverse. I need diversion, distortion, fog and blur to help me get through. I need to drink hard or drive fast or to blowtorch my face.
    I say, 'Christ.'
    I'm never in this little flat to do more than sleep. I hate this place. Nothing happens here. Nothing can be made to happen here. It's 3:14AM. This is when I'm meant to be in this place but I can't be here.
    I sit on my sofa and these legs are restless, knees jumping and shaking, my mind spiralling away from me, a neural funfair daring me to play each time I try to get a clear thought. I keep looking at the hat on the coffee table. Can I be certain it's the same one?
    I go, 'Am I sure?' and I remember Fiz's dead face, Mim's burned eyes, Raymond's gaping head.
    And that mannequin's beside me now. Its busted neck and murdered throat. I used to slay it every night in some weird revenge therapy, some grief struggle they don't tell you about, they don't advise. I killed it forever and now it just sits there dead every night, both of us staring at nothing, at each other. Tonight, right now, it feels deader than ever, and I can't be near it.
    'Okay,' I go, as if someone else is with me, 'I need to call the cops.'
    I need to tell them a man has been murdered. But how do you say a thing like that? How do you say it when you're sitting at home after leaving the place

where you saw the body? They'll record it and play it back, listen to it over and over when they find the dead man who raped my wife. They'll listen to it, think how they could play it in court, play it to the TV cameras when I'm convicted of his murder.

I say, trying to get my head straight, 'Okay. Okay. So what's just happened?'

Dagny killed Mim's father. Right? Is that the case here? Has that intruder gone and bashed a hole in my dead wife's rapist's head? Is that what we are dealing with here? Or what? Has she shot him? Was that a bullet hole or a hammer hole in Raymond's head?

No. I have to call the cops. I have to say there's a man dead, a hole in his head, and that I think that self-obsessed YouTuber Dagny O'Reilly did it. It'll all sound fine once I start talking, once I ring the number. It'll all come out naturally. It'll all be great.

The obstacle becomes the way.

I stand fast, that weirdo mannequin jumping like he's going to stand too. I look at him and he's not moving because he's not real and deader than ever. I stuff the hat in a pocket, pull on a coat. And what I'm doing is strange behaviour, just the kind the cops will be looking for when they find Raymond the Rapist. But I have to know for sure. I have to check this. Don't I? I'll write how I felt it was fair enough that I make myself certain before announcing to the cops, *'my dead wife's hat vanished from my office and I found it on his face and I know for sure it's hers because it had vanished from my office.'*

I bet I look suspicious as hell as I arrive, doing all this stealing around with my face drained of blood and that cap from the murder scene. I've got this suspiciously white hair anyway. I've got these remade

Did She See You?

nails, these unreal clothes like I'm trying to hide. Right now, I've got this clown head all tipped forward as I walk, a low glow sliding along and getting filmed by houses and cars and shops and doorbells all over the place.

In the office now, flicking on the big light. It looks different, unreal, too many dark surfaces trying to shine like a painting of the place it was. I look over the bookshelves, at the garbage queued up for sorting. There are the man-up books, the reframe crap, the snowflake melting tirades, all the stuff that says nothing changes if nothing changes. The hat's not here. So now my hands are turning things over, lifting them, rooting around in among wires and plugs and coins and instruction books and contact lenses and pendants and searching for the only thing that can render tonight untrue. But it's not here. Fiz's hat has gone from the office. The hat which is now in my pocket used to be right here where my hands are.

It's four something, four and a half or so, and I'm stripped, soaked, far out in the water, further than I've ever gone. And I'll write how I come here to the lethal place to get calm. I'll say I come here to be in control, to unpickle the streets from my body in nature's ooze, to get man's waste out, to know I'll leave more real than when I arrived. I'll say I come to the dirty, tough place to survive, to pay my respects to the wisdom within every drop. I'll be able to tell my readers how I come here to make sense of everything around me and that I'm here now because I can't find any at all.

I'll have to get back to the edge, to the sand and land, if I'm to write it all down. But part of me is saying hard I should think about staying here for too long, about letting it cling to me and letting me cling to it forever. I don't know if it's heart or head, if it's animal or logical, but some strong part's saying I should find a long ladder to rest on, pause there before climbing down as deep as I can go. But I won't. That's not what this place is for, not now. This place is repurposed, reworked, recycled. This is the solitude place where the free-think decisions get sorted and cleaned. This is where I'll man-the-fuck-up and from where I'll exit as the early birds walk their mutts before breakfast. I'll step out looking like a sea alien, like a done dishcloth, and they'll not know whether to call the cops or the ambulance. But I know my head will then be clear. Expect it. Expect that. I must expect everything is going to be fine, that I'll know what to say and do.

 Did Dagny film me? Was her video on when she held up that phone in that rancid house? Are all the secrets now so dead that even that moment could be hi-res, hi-def, highlighted? I've got to assume she filmed me. I've got to assume now she's always been filming me. For all I know I could have been live online in that house, live online every time we've met. She could have a vicious tiny camera in the strap of her backpack, in her glasses, her eyes.

 I'll get some headspace, focus on my breathing now, think it all through. By the time I climb out of this ancient slop I'll have worked my way around all the permutations, all the ideas.

 It's six and I'm drinking a leftover half bottle of barely sparkling water in the driver's seat of my Disco, my Frankenstein ride, my Loser Rover, my clown car. I've barely dried myself, am shivering, shaking with cold, but I am unsunk.

Did She See You?

A finger's placed lightly on the call button, 999 already plugged in. There are some missed calls, numbers meaning nothing to me. Maybe sales calls, maybe robots who feel sorry for me, maybe people who want to ask me if I want to help myself. I can't care. I'm ready now. Ready to talk to the endless state now. I look across the water, the wide, flat, black spew at the city's mouth and I'm wise enough now to know I should have stayed, should have challenged Dagny. But I didn't have the balls. I wasn't man enough to discuss the emergency with that little pop-up psycho.

My hand jumps, my whole body jerks.
The phone. Ringing. Dagny. Jesus Christ.
It's ringing.
Ringing.
Okay.
Breathe.
Man up. Man up. Man up.
Highest ever value.
'Hey,' she goes.
'What did you do?'
'You wanna meet for coffee?'
'What?'
'My treat?'
'Dagny,' and now, shouting, 'What did you do!?'
'Woah. Jeez. What? Me?'
'Christ,' I say, 'I'm calling the cops. I have to call the cops.'
'Good plan,' she says.
'You're insane. You're desperately insane, Dagny.'
'Okay,' she goes. 'Whatever.'
'Are you filming me? Are you recording this?'
'You're totally paranoid, dude.'
'Why are you calling me?'

'Mim's told me everything.'
'Told you what?'
'Everything.'
'Told you what?'
'The real reason why you ask her that thing, the real truth of what happened that night. She's told me all that stuff, dude.'
'What?'
I feel my hand rubbing hard on my forehead, don't remember putting it there.
I go, 'Bullshit. Bullshit, Dagny. You've never met her. It wasn't you. It was Raymond. It wasn't even you who visited.'
'You think I've never met her? Seriously?'
'I know you've never met her.'
She goes now, 'Okay, if you say so. And take the call, Denis.'
And the phone's shaking, wriggling, telling me someone else seeks to speak. And Dagny's gone, hung up.
I breathe, answer, too filled with confusion to have room to care who or what this is.
'Hello,' he says, 'this is Shadi from...'
'Shadi? What is it?'
'Yes,' he says, 'it is Shadi. From New Ready House.'
'I fucking know who you are. What is it?'
'Okay. Of course. It's early.'
'What is it? What?'
'I'm sorry to disturb you but the police are here.'
'Why?'
'I am obliged to let you know.'
'Why are the police there?'
'I'm afraid this news might come as a shock.'
'Just tell me, for fuck's sake!'

Did She See You?

'It's about Mim, or Miriam.'
'No shit. What about Mim?'
'She has gone. She is missing.'
'What?'
'She is missing, and we have called the police.'
'What?'
'She is...'
'Like, what? Escaped?'
'Yes. You could say she has escaped.'

My hand's shaking now, fingers dancing and holding this thing like it's burning. Is it because I'm too cold, too terrified, too confused? I'm overloaded, unable to process myself. I'm WALLOPED, ZONKED, SLAMMED, DAMNED, DONE.

I stop the silence, say, 'I don't have a word for this, Shadi. I don't know what to say.'

He says, 'Oh, that's okay, Mr Bic. So can you come please?'

And I'm thinking I know only one thing for sure right now. I know what he doesn't know. I know someone broke into Mim's father's skull and stole his life. I know that Dagny O'Reilly did it. Or now I know maybe Mim did it. Maybe Mim broke out of the nuthouse and broke into her father's head. I know someone did. I know that for sure. I feel like throwing up and I don't know how long it has been since I felt like throwing up.

Shadi's still talking. We're still on the phone here. He's saying something slow and flowing, something calm and clear and heavy and it's too much. I don't need it. I hang up. I listen to myself breathe out and watch the heat fall and pause on the windscreen, watch it pull away.

'No,' I say.

It wasn't Mim. Couldn't have been Mim. Mim couldn't have got that hat, could she? Only Dagny could've got that hat, stolen that hat. Mim couldn't have got to his house on her own, could she? Mim's brain is not level enough, is too broken, too buckled, whirring in useless squiggles, not spongy and reactive and experienced enough to adapt.
I call Dagny.
I cancel.
Unsure.
I call again.
It's ringing out.
The light rising, the creamy yellow of the sand getting clear, the hidden blue of the water, the secret green of the distance. A gnarled big ball of seaweed, a lump of wood or netting or a big dead fish on the beach. It's getting nudged by dainty little waves, long white lines gently knocking at it, over and over, then vanishing into the soft ground. I'm drawn to that thing, to how it's being made to make those small movements again and again by the water and how it stays in the same place. I'm drawn to its shape, its colours, to the way it's all so tightly bound by whatever it's been through, how it's packaged and unexplored, its natural greens and browns like lost camouflage. It's ready to explain its struggle to whoever visits first, to show how it got all mysterious from dead things. I can't be the one. I can't allow myself to look, can't let myself know if that is whoever it was. I can't be that guy right now. Don't absorb, observe.
'Jesus,' I say.
I fire up the engine, click in the belt, turn the wheel, release the brake, dig thick, cheap black rubber into the grain, spin off in another direction. I tell myself

Did She See You?

how I like the normalness of the sound of the vehicle, the surety of its progress.

Jason Johnson

Twenty

Assert: I nourish my mind and body daily.

SECURITY guards wave me into the car park and I'm looking around for cops. There are often police cars here yet now there are none. I'd have expected a line of them, a big splash of that white, yellow and blue because an asylum has lost a girl. Maybe they're all out there on the hunt for a killer, trying to track down a wayward waif described as a 'phenomenon' by an expert.

I walk to the security gate, face into the camera, get buzzed through, stride between the high wire fences, strut to the entrance, shoulders back. Deep breaths. Reframing. Acting as if. Taking nothing personally. All very high value and very unimpressed.

ID check. Sniff from a dog. No food, no drugs. A look in the eye, nod of a head.

A guy goes, like we're friends, 'Mr Bic.'

I glare a little. He needs to know I'm annoyed, in shock, horrified they've lost a person.

Dr Harriet, all nerdy and short legs and big fake specs and digital clipboard, is waiting. She looks over the top of the big rims, shows no emotion, maybe has none.

She reaches out and I reach back. A rare greeting meant to speak of sincerity and importance. I can feel from the way I do it, from my own shake, that I'm calmer now, better now, stronger now, higher value now. I don't care about Raymond, about who left him hole-headed and dead as a dildo in his bed. I don't care

Did She See You?

about Dagny and her bullshit videos. I'm all risen above. I'm only caring right now about Mim.

'This is an extraordinary event, Mr Bic,' she says.

My voice is businesslike, goes, 'No shit. How'd she get out?'

'She took an opportunity,' she says, her legs trying to keep up with my important pacing. 'It says quite a bit about her thinking...'

I barge in all righteous, go, 'Doesn't it just? Haven't I told you a thousand times that she's acting this whole thing?'

New Ready's security hive is roomy, comfortable, designed to make you feel okay as you watch people be about their business. Long walls up to state-of-the-art natural lighting, desks that glow a tinny, happy, burnt orange. All the sockets are silver, most of the screens are images of walkways, of pretty walls. The air-con is so good it's like air up a mountain, air over an iceberg. You could do yoga in here, slide into your downward dog and cobra as killers commute and maraud around on monitors. There are images alongside the screens, happy hand-drawn sketches of inmates and staff, pictures with names below, pencilled euphemisms from relaxed minds. They could be by staff or by clients, these pictures. They could be by both, be of both.

The coffee smells great and the team is delightful. This is just what you'd expect in this touchy-feely human experiment where the mad get a world, their own loving, free and blameless community where the only thing to do is exist.

Two detectives scroll through footage noting times, pointing at people, at timestamps, at green glows on big doors. They're zipping back and forward, full access to the unfolded story. I'm waiting for them to break away, to be introduced.

I say to Harriet, 'Any sightings?'

She nods towards the cops, says, 'They'll explain.'

I say, 'Okay. And I wanted to check something with you, to confront you really, Harriet. He arranged the visit through you? Isn't that right?'

'I'm sorry? Who?' she says.

'Mim's father. Who do you think?'

'Oh yes. I know that was disconcerting for you. However, I think our focus...'

'Did you allow his visit without researching his background?'

'Okay. It's not that simple. You want to talk about this now?'

'I want to talk about how far Mim might have gotten, to be honest. That's my priority. But right now, it looks like I have to wait. So, in the meantime, if you don't fucking mind, can you start to explain because it's clear to me that his visit has made her...'

'Mind your language.'

'Sorry.'

'I allowed his visit. Once he was able to prove who he was, once that was all confirmed by Mim's grandmother, then he had a right to apply and I had a right to permit his visit.'

'But I had no right to know?'

She turns away, turns back, fixes me, goes, 'There is no conviction against him, as you know. And there is documentation naming Mr Raymond Grull as Mim's biological father. He remains in contact with your late wife's family. I repeat, they had no objection to his visit.'

Louder, I go, 'Sorry, what?'

Did She See You?

Quieter, she goes, 'I could, Mr Bic, have refused him but I felt it had value and it is part of my role to add value to the lives of my patients. I do not need to explain myself. And I certainly don't believe I need to be explaining any of this right now.'

One cop turns, steps my way, shakes a hand. He's a chunk over six-foot, jaw as big and permanent as a listed building, a flat-nosed rugby menace in his day.

'DI Stables,' he says, Aussie accent, 'thanks for coming. Call me Al.'

'Denis,' I say. 'I need to know everything you know.'

'Of course. First thing is to say I've got a great team on the case, just so you know. Drones are up, we're covering all routes, gathering every scrap of CCTV. If she's on foot, and probably is, she's likely in the woods around here somewhere. There's a dog search ongoing, three-mile radius. Including private property. It's thorough. Be assured of that.'

'But you've not done this before though.'

'Not here, no. Not at New Ready House. Did she say anything to you recently? Anything to make you think she might make a run for it?'

'Nothing. She doesn't communicate in any normal sense. How'd she get out?'

He's about to answer when the other cop, phone to his ear, calls over.

'Al,' he says, 'get a look at this.'

Alan says, 'One sec, JP.'

He turns back to me.

'She walked out, mate,' he says, flicking his eyebrows. 'It was as simple as that. You could put it down to bad gatekeeping.'

'Walked out?'

And I sense Harriet cringing.

'She switched some clothes in plain sight with a visitor and walked out in the middle of a group of people. The visitor she'd met sat on, kept her head down. She made it look like she was Miriam and Miriam was her. Just flipped it, you could say. Hiding in plain sight. Hard trick to pull off, but your girl managed it. She did it even though there isn't a single fool in this building, mate. At least none of those here involuntarily.'

It all makes sense. The organisation of it. The clarity, the simple cleverness of it. The underestimation of her. She had thought it through. She found a path through the obstacle. And it hits me - I know where she's going.

The big cop puts a thick hand on my shoulder. He's been reading my face. And I have to run. I have to tell him I've to go right now. I'll say my iron's still on, my office is unlocked, that I need to lie down, need my meds or that...

He goes, 'I can tell it's unsettling for you, Mr Bic. And I know what you're going to ask next.'

I go, 'Yeah. It's okay if I go? I just need to get my head together. This is...'

He takes his hand away, shrugs, goes, 'Do what you need to do. We just need to be able to stay in contact with you. Do you have any thoughts on where she might want to go? Any persons or places that might be of interest?'

I shake my head, 'No,' I say, 'No,' trying to look like I mean it. And there's something serious hanging over this conversation. He said he knew what I would ask next and I haven't asked it.

I go, 'Who was the visitor?'

Did She See You?

He nods now, satisfied with the question.
He goes, 'Well that's the weird thing. We have the woman in custody and to be honest, we're just trying to make sense of it all at the moment.'
'Who is it?'
'She says she's Miriam's mother.'

Jason Johnson

Twenty-One

Assert: Forces all around will seek to pull you from your mission.

THE parties in that house were too long, too loud, too much. Raymond's capacity for vacuuming up drugs was incredible. He'd pack that house with ravers, tell the neighbours to get fucked and burn on like a jet engine for a dozen dawns and dusks. He was a cousin of Fiz's, a nephew to her wild-eyed father, a runt of a man so well connected with local thugs that he never suffered for anything he did. He never got shut down or kneecapped or beaten up in an area where that kind of thing has been part of the process for decades. What hamstrung Raymond the Rapist, in the end, was the partying itself. The vast and deep addiction to the massive buzz, the intense need to keep going, to conquer any stability, upping the doses into the night, into the day, week on week, month on month. No one can go on like that, endlessly spangled, their life disintegrating as they sail on three sheets and rudderless into the wind.

I'll not write much on this. I'll touch on it, but I'll be careful how I explain it all in the book. I'll not say how I met him through Fiz, that I started buying from him when I was low, that he knew just the right time to approach with a panacea for sale. I'll not be getting into how he ended up donating to me because there were times when my demand was bigger than my wallet.

I'll say nothing on why I'd avoided that master bedroom when I was upstairs in his house, about when I found him dead in the box room. Part of me thinks I

Did She See You?

should've entered the big bedroom, had a look, breathed it in and let the memories flow.

I'd lived in that house back then, all bliss and poison-powered, all bouncing and jumping and fighting among the parties, beyond the pain of being dumped hard by hardcore Fiz.

Raymond's wife Joan was in and out of jail at the time, in and out of relationships, sometimes taking in men for money, sometimes taking them in because they arrived at the door. I won't be writing anything about how many girls and guys ended up in that big double room in those crazy days. Less than half the people in and out of that place were less than half-aware of any kind of rules as the unwashed duvets got tangled up.

Reconnecting finally with Fiz and moving to that old stone house was everything. It was a move away from the discomfort of the user's life, a move two miles outside the city, up and beyond. Getting to a cleaner, quiet place filled a gap, gave me focus, got me sober, made me organised and ambitious. I owe all that to Fiz.

The old house was sold on by her late father's lawyer after Fiz died. It should have been mine in law, but such was the tension at the time I let it go. That house had been on the news many times, pictured in newspapers. A weird place, built backwards and facing up the slope, its back to the city. It was the grumpy, moody old rack where the loopy girl with the gangster grandfather shot her unhinged mother and climbed a tree. It was where the crazy kid in the branches aimed a gun at armed police, where she got close to getting shot dead herself.

That place sold for much less than it was worth yet had three times as many snap-happy viewers as anything similar on the market. There's a plan now to knock it down, to convert it into out-of-town studio apartments as the city climbs into the hills. But work on that has yet to begin, the initial detailed assessing and scouring of the land by environmental bodies is still to come. For now, it's much as it was, just a little more dilapidated, a little less loved.

I've been here many times, wandered around, peered through the front windows at the back, the back windows at the front. I've seen how that stone cottage with the cheap extension has been rifled through by nosy kids, how thieves have stripped copper wire and floorboards and sinks. That falling apart house, a questionable, damp legacy for Fiz from her father, is continuing its long journey of falling apart. Yet I feel no sadness when I see it.

Parked up outside now, I see again how the once wild hill around it looks washed clean, farmed, ordered and organised to the last inch. That contrast with the house, its Boston Ivy moving thickly inside and shrinking window holes like a pretty disease. I watch from the road as full sunshine rests on the rear of the place. And despite the slow, stealthy clogging and strangling, it still looks like a wonderful little home.

The state of your home is an exact reflection of the state of your mind.

Approaching on foot and there's not a sound, barely a chirp, hardly a rustle from the four-foot grass. I pass the little bathroom window at the side, a rectangle of opaque glass, the little steel stopper on the outside preventing a full opening, blocking escape. I push the black gate towards the hill, its single functioning hinge causing the scrape of wood against wood and I hope no one heard. A crow calls out as I go as if mimicking the sound.

Did She See You?

    This path along this left side of the house is almost gone, shrunk to a grey trickle by the tough, bullish green closing in from either side. The garden, rising with the hill, has been untended since I last cut it back two years ago. It's like a cheap safari here, an overgrown oasis of mild weather wildness on an otherwise tightly managed bank. The summer embellishments are claiming all the space they need, rushing to live freely on the otherwise tamed slope. A bird I don't see flies from somewhere close as I turn right, wading into the thickness, a half-track where unsolicited visitors on the climbing road have walked in search of goods, of kicks, of a place to pee or grope or hang out.

    I'm walking towards the big window where our living room was and squeeze my eyes to take it in. The glass cracked from the outside, almost everything inside removed. All that remains is that great mirror above the fireplace, bent at one side where someone tried to pull it down only to discover how resolutely it had been bolted to that wall. Maybe that same person chose to break it, to thump it in anger, watching themselves as they took revenge on the looking glass and saw themselves fracture. It's the mirror that carried the story of Fiz's death and I never wanted it, never claimed it when I came to take what was mine from this killing place.

    The back door's still there, sitting heavy and proud despite the busted lock and easy swing. The security camera above, our unblinking eye on Mim, is smashed, bending and fading away, greying out among the green along with the rest of this property before the surveyors arrive.

Jason Johnson

I keep my eyes on that glass in the living room, my blondeness like a stain on the surface, using it to see what's behind me. Some leaves are rising and falling in the small breeze, some branches shifting with delicate effort. There's a bee buzzing close by, a fly passing above my head. I look at the reflection of Mim's old oak and can't make anything out, the summer embellishment too rich to reveal what's inside. It's unclear but I can just about see what I'm sure is a little track to its trunk, a new, thin, barely visible trail and I know she's here.

I turn to face where she is and she'll be watching, expecting. I don't know what she's planning, if she has something – a stick, a stone, or more – to pound down if I come close. But I have to go to her. This is the time. It's here where the environment has changed and the pattern's been interrupted. This is the time to ask her.

My legs are damp, jeans soaking up dew as I step onwards into the deep back garden. I look up, needing her to know I'm coming, needing her to know I know she's there. I join her meek route, follow the evidence of her sad little journey back to where things must have somehow made sense to her. And I hear her now clothing the silence with little taps on wood, little words. I hear the nervous energy of her mind forcing her to make a million moves and think a million things. Ten feet from the trunk and I stop, look way up into the dark and crisscrossing brown bent bones.

'Hi Mim,' I say.

And the tapping's still going as I catch the whispering now. Words racing, beating a rhythm, a thin layer of audio over the summer quiet. I walk a little closer, along what's left of her fresh path, and look up further, to almost the top of the great tree.

Did She See You?

Tapping, whispering, a little bare foot neatly swinging, scarred toes furling and unfurling. An escaped fugitive, a KILLER, a MONSTER, a PSYCHO, a BEAST, shoeless and up a tree, saying little words she's pretending are arriving in her brain from your friend, your mum, your partner, your bank. She's wearing jeans, a white top and is as pale and thin as a skinned twig. I walk even closer to the bare ground around the trunk now, among the little rocks and stones she'd dropped like small bombs in the past. And, as the sun falls warmly down from above her, I can see the face, a blurred dot aimed at me, eyes like drops of tar, her whole presence somehow alien. The mouth's moving, the hands drumming, the eyes rigid.

I say it slowly, holding that eye contact we never have, never had. I say, 'Did she see you?'

Tapping, drumming, racing, watching and ignoring.

'Did she see you?'

Whispering, words rolling along, can't make them out.

'Mim?'

Whispering, rapping, speeding it up a little.

'Did she see you?'

Hearing precise words in there, more defined, but too quiet to identify, too light from her always-on lips to make out.

'Mim,' I say, 'is that why you came here?'

Still no blinking but tapping hands, that easy swinging foot.

'Is it?'

And I'm picking up on a measured move up the gears, her talent to hold the integrity of the syllables while increasing the pace.

'Is that why you came here?'
Ticking along fine now, fast and smooth.
'To check?'
Flying along, but contained, controlled, confident.
'Will we check now?'
And stop. She's stopped. Frozen. It's astonishing. Something has stopped. Nothing has started. Our Trouble has astonished me with nothing.

I swallow hard, nervous, suddenly out of my depth. Here it is. Here's that moment. The pause. The break. The chance. Is it now?

I go, 'Did she see you?'
And she stares.
I go, 'Will we check now? Will we? Let's check, see if she saw you, okay? Then we'll know once and for all. That's all. Then you're free. Okay? How does that sound?'

Still silent. Still fixed on me. It's like a glitch in the matrix, this still gargoyle among these breathing branches.

Her legs, over that branch, draw closer together, cross at the shins now. She starts to lean forwards, tilting downwards, about to plunge my way, dive headfirst thirty feet and I don't know what to do. She goes on tilting, her legs squeezing the branch and I fear now for her life. She's holding on, turning more, hanging upside down, a monkey doing some kind of trick. I don't know if those stick legs can hold her, if she truly wants to drop or dive-bomb or die. Her head hanging now, dry hair waving, neck stretched, those troubled, burned eyes upside down and on me.

'Mim don't,' I say.

She turns to the underside of the branch, squeezes a hand into an unseeable little cavern in the bark. She

Did She See You?

pulls it out now, a black plastic bag, a bin liner wrapped tight.

Retrieved, she swings herself deftly back to the top of the branch.

And there it is.

I lift my arms, go, 'I've a charger in the car, Mim. Drop it down, please. Drop it down.'

My hands are out, ready to catch.

'Then we'll know,' I say. 'Drop it down. Please. Please.'

She's looking at me, her little dancing beggar saying 'please.' She's saying nothing, not moving at all, as if growing stable from seeing me at my weakest.

'Miriam,' I say, wanting her to think my way now, using that little cheat code to convince her she'd said something, done something. I go, 'Drop the phone like you said you would. Remember you said you would? You said you would.'

And there's another foot, an all-new foot behind Mim's. Two new feet are emerging from the leaves as Dagny O'Reilly shuffles along from the bushy end of the same branch, two new feet in shiny pink boots. That round face, smiling, blinking. Jet-black hair so glossy it's mimicking the green around her, holding that sunbeam from above. Mim doesn't move, isn't motivated at all by the arrival of this digital thug in mirror shades to her side. And, ignoring us both, she starts talking again, whispering all the words coming up over the hill.

Dagny goes, those picture eyes right on me, 'Don't Mim, don't you give him that.'

And I'm so fucked off and I go, 'Dagny, for Christ's...'

'She won't,' says Dagny. 'You know she won't give it up. Not to you. Of all people. You can try to convince

her she said she would, but she won't. I know all about you trying to convince her she's done something she hasn't. I've learned all about that, dude.'
'Dagny,' I say.
And the bloated millionaire, backpack straps looped over shoulders, bends the branch as she moves closer now, pressing into Mim's space like she's trying to shove her towards the trunk, to push the quiet babbler out of the way. She stretches out a fat right leg, swings it back so it strikes Mim's left foot, body language suggesting she has some unhealthy plan for this fugitive.
I go, cautious, firm, 'What's going on, Dagny? What's your plan up there?'
And she laughs, turning to look at Mim and then back to me. She bends an ear now, twists her head as if listening to every word from the troubled killer, nods her head as if it's all making sense, as if she's agreeing with all Mim says.
Dagny goes, 'Mim and I are both thinking you're thinking *"gee that damn YouTuber probably never climbed a tree before."* And are we right?'
I nod, say, 'Whatever. Just come on down, Dagny. It isn't safe for both of you there.'
She goes, 'Well, we got some great trees where I come from. You can do, like, a tour of the Redwoods, you know. Ever hear of California Redwoods, Dense?'
And I can just make out how Mim's picking up on the words, reflecting what her new friend's saying, going all, *'...redwoods in California where stream inside its basketball boots persist don't tell stories of dissenter hill Belfast run studio crow DI Stables...'*
Dagny goes, 'And man, those damn trees are the best. The best! I've climbed a Redwood in my time,

Did She See You?

buddy, oh yeah. Needed a little help to get started but once I was on that tree, I was like an arborist, man.'

She swings her legs hard like kicks, goes, 'I was stabbing boot blades right into that big old thing and rising up. So don't you go thinking a little anaemic Irish oak on some pissy little hill is going to freak me out.'

And she's leaning on Our Trouble now, pushing her even though scrawny Mim's so precarious on that branch, even though there's too far to fall, too many hard tree limbs to strike on the way down.

Dagny goes, 'The things I've done, Denis. You'd be surprised. If you think climbing a tree is something, you haven't understood at all, you know.'

'Okay,' I say, agreeing with her, thinking I need to play this so very carefully right now, thinking the craziest one up that tree might not be the escaped lunatic. I go, 'Whatever you say, Dagny. I'll do your show, whatever you want.'

She goes, 'Too late for that, dude. Too late for that. Overtaken by events. Your story became my investigation, you see, and Mim's the interviewee now. You get me?'

And I'm nodding, saying, 'Yes. I get you. And that's fine. I just want to make sure Mim's going to be okay, you understand?'

'Mim's fine,' she says, 'can't you hear? All is normal for Mim. If you care about Mim then your priority should be to consider that you have something to confess, don't you think? Just for her wellbeing.'

And I'm just agreeing, accepting it all, the beggar below boxed in a trap. The threat to Mim seems so clear yet Mim doesn't get it, maybe can't get it. Has she fallen for the digital diva, for the savage brightness of her trashy peacocking, for the strong currents of her chat, for the intensity of her symmetry, the curious density of her flesh and bone?

'So,' says Dagny, 'here's what I think...'

And I want to let rage reign, to scale my way up that tree and scream in her face, shove her from the branch.

She goes, '...it's time you said what was what. Am I right?'

And Mim's muttering about it being time to admit everything and Dagny's going, '...to say it right here, okay? Say it now, okay?'

And she's pressed against Mim now, squeezed so unnecessarily hard. A sudden movement could send the stick girl plunging into that bad, timber filter. I'd try to catch her. If she does, I'll try to catch her. I'm ready to try to catch her.

Dagny goes, 'So clarify please. For Mim.'

And I go, 'Yes.'

She goes, 'Then do it.'

And my arms are ready to reach out and I go, 'I will.'

She says, 'So say it.'

And I will. I will.

I pause, a one-second gap, then reach deep for the truth, clear my throat, go, 'Mim didn't shoot her mother, okay? Okay, Dagny? Is that okay?'

And it's like my muscles are being sucked into my bones like I'm tensing hard and tight ready to catch a girl from gravity, a lost human tumbling and crashing down from her place of hope. And I've said the words, flipped the story.

Dagny goes, 'That lie of yours has been the story you wanted to tell everyone, even tell yourself. Isn't that

Did She See You?

right, Denis? You almost convinced yourself that Mim shot her that night, didn't you?'

I go, 'Yes. Yes, Dagny. You take care up there, okay?'

She eases now, splits from Mim as if removing the threat to steal her seat on the crammed branch. And she's bracing now, as if ready to return, lifting her hands as if ready to slam back and shove Our Trouble into the air and I'm there, ready, arms now out and I know Dagny is relishing this anguish.

But it's Mim now, Mim who's leaning away. It's Mim loading up, gathering strength, getting louder now, going, '...*alien mental killer liar thief wrecker beast idiot trouble story dense...*'

It's Mim now, Mim ready to fight, Mim raising her arms, balling her fists and turning to Dagny. It's Mim who slams hardest, who bangs into the visitor, who forces her big hard butt to slip from the branch, who clenches her face and pushes her hands as, with a scream, Dagny falls.

And it's a thump into one branch, into two, three, four. It's a face slap into the trunk. And into the open air she comes as I watch, all in slow motion, as she lands on her head, neck wrenched.

And in that one moment, my arms all locked to catch, standing in the wrong place and way too late, I've failed. I've refused to do what I could, not even tried. I've been too scared, too stunned, too weak to do the right thing and I've been so busy observing I've not even tried. Now, this new crime, this twisted horror, its back cranked over its backpack, its neck jack-knifed, its already-bruised face deathly, glasses fractured, black eyes beneath. And there's no comfort here, no victory or goal achieved, just more problems, more madness. I let my arms drop and I don't know who I am anymore.

   I look at this child prodigy, this other phenomenon, and I hear soft steps now, the determined walking, his pacing through the hushing grass. He's come from over the hedge, from a neat field into this unruly garden. He's closing in from behind, the cadence of his big plodding unbroken by any location, any nature, any obstacle. And he's grief today or guilt today or both of those things and I don't know what he knows and I don't know what he wants but when he shows he wins. I just want to rise against his plan, to turn, to swing my pointless arms at him, to look up and scream into that washed away face no one but me has seen. But as he comes, he steals the energy from everything so fast. He switches it all off, all the sound, the pictures, all the pulse of the world. His truest power is that he unleashes an enormous pause when you need to advance, sticks you where you are and claims your full attention, comes right in close to your new stop to say things that crush a heart.

   And I need to get up this tree now, to get to her. I need to get up, to tell her it's okay, to get that phone, get the true recorded story of that night. I need to keep these eyes open, to not let him draw that thick sheet over my head. I need to get right up to tell her I know she didn't kill her mother, that she must always know she didn't kill her mother, that the trick was to help her, was all for her, that we love her. And he's whispering in my ear now about Fiz doing nothing wrong, how she used to leave me little notes and tell me I've gold bones. He says she was too good for me, always too good for me, says the truth is that I was the one who killed her, that I still haven't learned a thing and I feel like crumbling down at the foot of this tree.

But he's not there, never there, and I must make myself know it. He's not there because he's here, right in me, in my head, busy grabbing and biting and tearing at emotions and memories. It's me versus me here, the only real fight there ever is.

And I'm high value now, superhuman now and fighting off his cargo of grief, blocking it out of my head, making noises, growling, cursing, shouting, talking, thinking everything, babbling anything I can as I pull from his misery resin. I shout to myself that I'm full of bounce and drive and noise and focus and I'm trying to climb now, ignoring how he rises with me, a wicked invisible parasite heavy on my back. I'm reaching for another branch and ascending and refusing the black sky he'll pull over me and I look up and she's gone, a bare foot rising further into the tree.

My shoe slips, now a hand and I fall further than I knew I'd climbed and he's backing away, moving across the garden, off into the field with his words on Fiz, with my stolen thoughts on his low mind. I've beaten the bastard and as I look up in slow motion into the branches my back hits the ground, an all-over punch, wind and blood forced hard from my mouth, my nose.

And she shouts down, invisible in the treetop now, *'...alien mental killer liar thief wrecker beast beautiful run idiot persist persist trouble trouble trouble did she see you did she see you...'*

She's going, *'...manipulator psychopath bastard heartless trouble trouble Fiz bang run run did she see you did she see you...'*

And my eyes are closing and she's going, *'...did she see YOU did she see YOU did she see YOU did she see YOU...'*

I don't know how broken I am and I'm trying to stand as she's yelling, *'...did she see YOU did she see YOU did she see YOU did she see YOU...'*

I can smell the blood, feel it on my face, in my hair. It feels like it's pouring out as I try to stand, world rolling in all directions.

And she's shouting, *'...did she see YOU did she see YOU did she see YOU did she see YOU...'* and I'm saying, 'Man up. Fight back. Not dead can't quit. Not dead can't quit.'

I look at Dagny, her busted neck, eyes half-closed, and I call, 'Mim.'

I call the name over her repetition, over her line, her ongoing shout, over the lying question no one will hear. And I'm on my knees, staring into broken mirrors, into those half eyes, one brown, one blue, a shattered symmetry.

I call it out more, 'Mim, Mim, Mim...' and I look up but there's nothing, she's vanished, gone right to the top, to stay, to stop, maybe to sleep up there once more, maybe to live there for as long as she can.

I look down again and the eyes are more open now. There's a rattle in the throat now, some muscle moving. Dagny's alive. She's alive and I can't let her die.

I shout, 'I'm taking her. I have to take her, Mim.'

And I don't know if I'm weak or strong anymore, if my bones are broken or my blood is leaking bad. But I lift her, California's cutest fatberg. I place her over my shoulder, ready to go. And a rustle from above, a slap, a shiver and I look up, sunbeams jagging into my eyes. Something's coming and I don't know what. And I'm ready to try to catch it. This weight on my back and I'm trying to get whatever is falling. And that black plastic bag comes plunging and bouncing off two, three branches, out into the open air and right into my hands as the near dead girl on me stays where she is.

It takes me just seconds to kick the door into that trespassed property. I carry Dagny, a shortcut straight through the house to the Disco. I look along the corridor where we lived, see the peeling walls and carpet pissed on by strangers and vandals and thieves, see a word scraped into the plaster under a window and it reads *Persist*.

I see into the living room, to where Fiz died, see the cracked mirror as I go, see my face as I ferry Mim's crime through the flipped house from the front to the back. I carry Dagny to the car, open a rear door, lay her down, close it over, try to save a life, but I'm sure as I look at her it's already too late.

Twenty-Two

Assert: All beauty comes from struggle.

EYES alive, checking mirrors, speed, everything in sight. Need to be on my game, consistent focus. Am far from out of danger here. Far from safe. The eye of an emergency. Don Henley's *Dirty Laundry* on the stereo and hands sticky with blood on the wheel and I don't know if what I'm doing is right or wrong.

Mim's iPhone is dead but it's plugged in and charging. Just need a few per cent to know what untellable truth it recorded before it's gone forever.

There's a terrible silence behind, a still lump of former full-on life on the back seat. Dagny's pulse had gone, her breathing stopped, her eyes dead by the time I laid her down.

I call Bet.

'Denis?'
'I need help.'
'Mim's escaped. It's on the news.'
'Yes.'
'Where are you?'
'I need help.'
'Of course. Are you safe?'
'I'm safe. I found her.'
'Where?'
'Will you go to the old house.'
'Okay.'
'Go into the garden, to the big oak I told you about.'
'Okay.'

Did She See You?

'Mim's there. In the tree. At the top. Don't let her out of your sight.'

'And you?'

'She has killed someone.'

'What? Who?'

'The one I told you about. The YouTube one. Dagny O'Reilly.'

'Oh my god.'

'I know.'

'How? Where?'

'I have Dagny in the car. I was going to take her to hospital but... she died. I was carrying her, and she died.'

'We'll sort this. Where are you taking her?'

'She was with Mim and me and now she's dead.'

And I'm seeking the emotion I need, the attitude I need, the courage, the balls, the guts that Fiz would have told me to have.

Bet says, 'Where are you now, Denis?'

I go, 'I'm handling it. Let me handle this for Mim, for Fiz. Just go to her, please. Just go and wait there, at the tree, make sure she's safe. If the police come looking for her, just say you found her and show them, okay? Don't talk about Dagny, okay? She was never there, okay?'

'Okay, okay. Trust me.'

'I trust you.'

'And what are you going to do, Denis?'

'I have to do this for Mim. I have to make this story right. For Mim.'

'Stop and think, Denis. I have to say that to you. Wherever you are, just stop. Just pull over and think this through.'

'No, Bet. No. Go and make sure Mim's okay, right? Make sure she goes nowhere.'

I hang up, turn up the music, try to breathe, clear the head, feel the moment, feel the grain of the wheel in my sticky hands, the push of the seat in my back, the roll of the engine under my feet. I press the pedal a little more, closing in on Quarrel Bay.

Fiz had been all over the place when she became Raymond's victim. She'd been on a drug binge for weeks, maybe months. I'd been a mess too, just moved into Raymond's house, wasting my days. He'd told me his cousin Fiz had been coming around, that my ex had been begging him for any gear he could offer, how she'd been living in some hellhole squat and plunging needles into her arms. He said she'd flipped, become dependent and weak and afraid and sluggish and ugly, become the opposite of herself. He said her family had stepped away from her in the same way they had ditched him, that her grandmother Freda was the only one left to love her.

He laughed when he said she'd walked away from all the promise and hope and expectation a person could be lucky enough to have. He said it was funny that no one cared about her anymore and that she had made the worst available decisions. I told him I no longer gave a shit about her and he said I was right and we climbed high and sank low that night.

I saw her days later as she made her way along the street to Raymond's, all meek and pale and undone and directionless save for that drive to get her fix. It was like someone else had taken over, some kind of shadow had come forward to pollute and dull her shine from the inside out. I'd been drinking and sniffing with Joan and the two of us looked through the doorway as, eyes closed, Fiz stood on the street all rubber boned and junkie hustle and begged Raymond for gear. He took that wasted woman inside and upstairs to that master bedroom, my room, to help push a needle into her because, he said, he'd help her out because she was family.

And in that moment, something seized me, something disturbed, or jealous, something angry and hollow, an awful falling that offered a whole new sensation by making me do nothing, making me not act, making me get out of the way of events. Its power was strong and bad and wrong and intense, and Joan and I fell into each other and became something I never wanted to be on that sofa.

I think how a million blinking spots of light would have swirled in Fiz's brain as Joan and I bit and spat and rolled and worked at breaking and insulting the last parts of who we'd ever been. I think now how every fibre in Fiz's body was caressed by the sweet concoction as Raymond struck out and used her all up with his needle and his mouth and his violence. I remember how he let rip with a roar signalling the climax of his awful victory as her addiction sang lies in her mind.

In time, numbed with guilt, at the edge of my sanity, I'd called her family, told them she was too far off-the-rails, and they said they knew. I said how she was one step from being sold beyond return and they said they blamed me for it all, for being the common factor in all of the decisions through which she lost her way. They said we were as lost and broken and insane as each other.

I check my speed, check my mirrors, glance down at Mim's phone, ease up on the accelerator. Pulling off the road, pulling into the beach now, down the little bumpy lane behind the trees. No one. No dog walkers, swimmers, no one. A huge cargo ship making its grey way from the Port of Belfast, a dumpy ferry arriving from the opposite way.

Two per cent on the old phone now. It's slow to boot-up but I don't blame it. It's been in a tree for two years. It gets there, opens its bright face as my eyes scan land, sand and sea for signs of life. I look for video files and a tiny voice in my mind is going, *'...did she see you did she see you did she see you...'*

The final film. Less than a minute long. I view it and know now for sure it could have destroyed the most precious parts of us all.

A minute later and I'm stripped with the late and weighty Dagny O'Reilly over my shoulder, the phone pushed into her pocket. I take her to the water's edge, ready to react fast, to pretend we're just some crazy people playing if anyone arrives. I walk her into the cold wet, her round, painted head hanging, her face smearing and tapping my chest.

I step into the brine, feel it drag on my shins and surround my torso. So unwelcoming at first and then so hard to leave. I share her with this victim, let it lift her as I begin to swim with another in tow. I lock one of her arms under my chin now and pull hard out into the deep and the little voice keeps saying, *'...did she see you did she see you did she see you...'*

We head towards the shipping lane and I calculate how, if I'm strong enough, that sailing lump of iron could cross our path. If I aim it right, give it all I've got, we could even arrive at its rear, try to drop down and get drawn in, get all churned up into chunks of meat for the fish. I tread water and it's using me up fast and I pull the phone from her pocket. I turn it over in one hand, over and over, gasping and failing and looking at this

Did She See You?

little black rectangle, this thing I've sought all this time. I press play on that video once more, once more out here among the truth and honesty. And again it unspools that most secret evidence. Even now in the wet, it still holds the events of that night, the truth of the minute that ended with the hole in my wife's head, with the fact of Mim's innocence.

I turn my palm over once more, as if to lie the device on the surface of the sea. And for a moment that sturdy thing seems to stop, to valiantly attempt to perch before the water embraces fast and sucks it down, the video restarting as that amazing machine of the connected drops to the sludge and bedrock, to be unplugged forever.

In my ear it's, '*...did she see you did she see you did she see you...*'

I swim further, need to put space between these two goodbyes. I tuck her thick arm under my chin once more and I'm shaking with exhaustion and I'm all salt and phlegm in the mouth, all sore and empty and tears in the eyes. In one hundred seconds it feels far enough to say goodbye to this foreign puzzle, this most relentless intruder into my life. It feels far enough now to ensure she'll be lost for days if not longer, if not forever. It's far enough for her to be eaten and swollen and rotten enough for her real story never to be told, for her to be bandaged and snagged by seaweed, to be scraped and drawn out of the big mouth of the lough and into the Irish Sea. The suicide brigade who come here so often don't come far enough, aren't strong enough or brave enough to truly challenge these waters. That's why they end up back on the beach so fast, why they end up dead and intact on some nearby shore.

And it's on repeat, being whispered right into my head and I don't know if it will ever end, '...*did she see you did she see you did she see you...*'

I just need to move her along, float her away, send her into big water between all the islands. I say to myself I can do this, that I must do this, that there's no choice now and I'm high value and I will succeed in this because I am doing the right thing.

I roll Dagny in front of me, look at her face, at her new bruised skin in the rainbow oils of the sea. I consider the death of a digital phenomenon in faraway bleak waters, the anguish of millions of subscribers, the evergreen story of the life, career and tragic self-death of Dagny O'Reilly.

'Bye Dagny O'Reilly,' I say, rasping it, trying to fill my beaten lungs, 'I'm sorry.'

I let her go, her face still and falling, given over to the sea's open tomb.

'*...she see you did she see you did she see you did she see you...*'

The words had been on a loop in my mind, constantly refreshed, as if into my head from the outside. But now they've gone. Now they've stopped. Now there's space in my brain and I don't know what to do with it.

The Californian face slowly sinks and I see bubbles at her mouth. I see her crazy eyes burst open, her white lips moving fast now. I see white eyes and a burned face. And it's just like Mim now, like Mim fading fast, disappearing from view, down and beyond. It's so like Our Trouble now, the thin girl, the mad girl, the talking girl still talking but doing that thing she so rarely does and looking right at me.

And it is.

Did She See You?

And I look again now. And it is.
This girl is Mim.
I shove my face into the water, stretch my eyes as far as they'll go and it's Mim going deeper, mumbling, sinking, darkness winning over her ghostly face.
I push my head in more, kick my legs up. An explosion of energy stolen from nowhere. I dive. Follow her, my eyes hard staring, brain repeating over and over that this is Mim who is sinking here, Mim who is drowning here, that I've dropped the wrong girl into the sea. This isn't Dagny, for Christ's sake. This isn't anyone else in the world but Mim. It's Fiz's daughter I'm reaching for, the girl she loved is slowly tumbling down and I cannot let it happen.
I cannot have this and I have to get her.
And it's a blur - the close horizon, its lines of land and sea, that dash of beach, that mob of bushes. The big still sea beneath me, in front of me, behind. Everything's a blur. The world would be clearer, plainer, simpler if I just closed these eyes. But I aim at the blur, the coastline a finish line, a lifeline, and I pull an arm, use all I've got to kick a leg, to drag a shoulder.
And the coast waits, comes no closer as I swim more, grit teeth, force foul potion from my mouth, keep my eyes on where I'm going and it's all fading and we're sinking. Seeing only Fiz now, how she was on that night, how she looked when last alive.
She'd been declining for weeks, months, before then.
The demons – her undone family, her haunting addictions, her increasing violence, her depressed husband, her insane daughter. It had been taking ownership of her, eating into the last space of her mind. She'd become angrier, hated how she was lashing out at

the world, at her own face, at me. She was paranoid, jumpy, talking to herself, forgetting to wash, refusing to eat, always feeling the world was watching, waiting for Mim to fuck it all up again. She was crashing down hard yet in the minutes when she was finally able to get a grip, she gripped hard and didn't let go.

She made the decision and did not doubt herself. She said it was the right move for her, for Mim, for me, and she told me how she wanted only, at last, to do the right thing for the family.

It was Fiz who stole that gun from Roddy, put it to her head in front of our eyes. We watched as she closed her eyes and took that ferocious direct action to, as she saw it, fix our lives. For her, in a moment of bloody, practical clarity, the obstacle of death was the way forward. She was losing her mind, told me of wanting to release the bruising madness filling her brain, emptying her heart. She'd been on the edge of killing her daughter, had been punching her husband when awake and asleep, said we'd travelled this hard road for long enough and it was time for change.

She had said, 'I need you to man up, Denis. I need you to stand in your truth, to know that my words mean things.'

She had said to me, 'Sometimes you have to do difficult things to make sure things are right.'

She had said, 'Life's a battle' and 'sacrifice assures progress' and 'you must be in control of your emotions or be at their mercy' and I had to 'get a grip' and 'man up and man up some more.'

It was like she had come back for a final fight against the forces pulling her apart and I refused to accept. As she drew up her plans days before, as I tried to think of ways to steer her from herself, she said she

Did She See You?

was going to secure a weapon and I told her she must not do that. She said, 'You will wear a glove and you will be forthright and single-minded as you collect the fired weapon from my hand. Do you understand me?' And I rejected it, told her to leave, told her to run away, to leave us if she had to, but to stay alive.

She said, 'You will put on the safety catch, take the weapon to Mim and place it in her right hand. You will tell her from that moment, over and over again, that she did it, that she killed me. You will imprint it on her mind, and she will form her thinking around that and you know that this will do her no damage because she will not care.

'You will continue to press that thought on her as she tries to get away from you on the occasion of my death. You will shout it at her and send her running from you.

'Once she has held that weapon, whether she drops it or not, it will be enough. Once she has placed herself in her tree, as she most certainly will, you will call the police. Do you understand me? Do you understand how I am taking control of this situation now and that I will not allow you to deny me the right to take that control? Do you understand me?'

She said she would cover her hand before pulling the trigger, that the cover would have gunshot residue. I was to take that cover, cut it up and flush it away along with the glove I had worn. She had lied to me about her hand being injured some days before. The bandage she had dressed that non-existent wound with was the cover I was to destroy.

Fiz said that, when the police interviews began, I would know the story to tell, that I already had the truth in my mind, that a blameless girl had changed everything.

She said, 'Consider this my will, Denis. My will is my choice and mine alone and I absolutely fucking insist you honour it. I know you and this is how my story ends. Do you understand me?'

I said I would not do what she asked.

She knew Mim would go to New Ready House, that state-of-the-art new centre for the criminally insane, that new place for the broken to go to be cherished for their fractions, that internationally funded testbed facility with standards beyond that of any household, any jail, any care home anywhere. Mim was young, intelligently crazy, her madness always written all over her face, always spilling from her mouth. She was an exceptional case ripe for exploration by one of the unquestionable talents that populated their rotas. There was nowhere better or safer for Mim to live out her days.

Fiz told me, 'I will have been a victim of someone else, not of my own hand. You will not be a suspect in my death. Bury me, know that it is my will and live again. Become what you need to become. Do you understand me?'

And I put my hands to my ears and yelled that she was mad, that there was no gun. I said she could not get a gun, that she must never get a gun, that no one would help her get a gun.

She was, she said, compelled to die on the hill on which she always claimed to stand. She said how she believed in sacrifice, that she demanded her right to do all she had detailed and that she had the courage required to finish the job and that my loyalty was more vital now than ever.

Did She See You?

  She said, 'I am desperately unwell, Denis. Do you see how unwell I have been? How violently unwell? How filled with demons I am? Have you seen it? Have you felt it? Have you recognised it for what it is?'
  And I knew it was true, but I would not accept her solution.
  She said, 'When you hand her the gun, when she's processing all she can about what happened to me, start it, implant it, imprint it and do not stop. Tell her she did it. Tell her you want to know the details of what happened. Tell her only she knows. Say it – did she see you? Say it over and over – did she see you? For this is the only way to ensure Mim gets what she needs.'
  She said, 'Do you understand me, Denis?'
  I said, 'There is no gun and I will not do this.'
  She said, 'Say it.'
  I said, 'I won't.'
  She said, 'Did she see you?'
  I said, 'No.'
  She said, 'Say it again and again.'
  I said, 'No. No. No.'
  She said, 'Did she see you, did she see you, did she see you, did she see you?'
  She said, 'You will keep saying it to her after my death. When she thinks of that moment, when she is in the moment of my death, whatever it means to her, will you keep ensuring you include her directly? It keeps you from it, places her in it. Do you understand me?'
  I said, 'This is not how it ends.'
  She said, 'I am telling you what you will say because this is what will save you, this is how you and I become free and how Mim becomes cared for and you must do it. This is how I do what's right for my family. This is how I am going to fix the mess I have made of all

of our lives. This is my duty. I will die for my family, Denis, and you do not have the power to stop me.'
I said, 'No.'
She said, 'Say it.'
I said, 'No.'
She went, 'You will.'
I said, 'I won't.'
She said, 'Hang for you, baby.'
I told her I'd die without her and she said I must not because I was responsible for myself. I told her she was brilliantly alive and she said I must remember it that way. She said that my story of what was about to happen was the only story the world could hold of her and that I must tell it and no other.

I didn't know it was coming that night. I hadn't factored in Roddy's arrival, had no idea he carried a weapon, had no idea it was taken from his bag that day. I'm not sure I ever believed she really would do what she had said but I know I should have known.

Fiz hadn't factored in the video, the recording underway as I arrived to see Mim standing at the door. Mim watching Fiz, Fiz with her back to us both, her face in the mirror. Fiz with the weapon at her temple, Mim's arm raised, pointing at her, collecting it all through a lens. The mirror reflected everything - the three of us pausing in a terrible moment. And Fiz took Mim's eyes, took mine, then took the decision she had already promised to herself and took her own life.

Mim had stood still as I'd removed the bandage from Fiz, used it to pick up the weapon in my unreal world. I'd clicked on the safety catch, taken the pistol to Mim, pressed it into her palm to secure her prints. Then, struck by the massive unusualness of the moments, she sprung to life. Before I could remove the gun again,

Did She See You?

before I could get the phone from her other hand, she began hitting out at me, striking hard, knocked me right over, rushed outside to the garden, scaled her tree. And I would never be able to find that phone.

'Did she see you?' was to imprint what she didn't know she hadn't done. And 'Did she see you?' became a way to break through once the imprint was confirmed, to get Mim to need to know the same answer too. Day by day I wanted to break her down, to force her to reveal the location of that phone so I could see what it had seen, so Mim could shut me up, so she could be left alone.

'Did she see you?' became my mantra, my endless noise, my scraping and digging and pushing as I sought to locate and remove that thing's story from the story of the world.

I wanted the phone's existence gone. I feared it would be found by police, by the army of environmental inspectors, surveyors, builders, planners due to begin work on the site. I wanted it gone because immense sacrifice demands extraordinary respect. I wanted it gone because the live death of my haunted wife could not be left to lie like a dead secret on a dirty hill, her most secret moment stuck in the muck, poised for some future misinterpretation, for some oncoming insult.

I'd searched every part of that land. I'd taken a metal detector over every inch. Only one person alive knew where it could be. The only tool I had to find it was persistence.

And the words to unlock that knowledge are with me now, the words to rewrite all of our stories are here again, light as a vanishing secret in my ear, Mim's whisper over and over and over.

Jason Johnson

'...she see you did she see you did she see you did she see you did she see you...'

And I'm not fighting this ocean now, not fighting nature, not fighting the world and myself to reach that vanishing blur anymore. My head's dipping in and out of the brine, my mind in and out of clarity. My muscles have no sensation to offer, dead meat skewered by heavy gold bones. I'm barely strong enough to cough and I'm breathing in the salty poison. And the eyelids won't discuss it anymore, the legs won't debate it. The lungs are bags of water now. Weight's gathering fast, stone by stone, heavier and heavier, a long tonne of me now visualising that ladder in the sea, wanting to rest on a rung and soon step downwards to the softness below. And it's all sinking now, all dropping, an ambrosia of down sensations, all going beneath now. No more stamping and swimming, no more breathing, no more whispers, no more journey. This is where all of us swimmers go, where we all go on our way back to our lost origins.

And my arms are around her, pulling her close with the last work of my heartbeats, head pressed to her head. My energy ended, we twist together in the great wet silence and slowly fall home.

Miriam – Three of Three

…'Run.'

His expectant ear waits.

But the sound cannot break through. The water between them is turning to sludge. It is tightening, gripping now, squeezing her torso, her head, crushing her throat, and the word is trapped where she said it.

And the blushed light dims and the strange tomb closes in and this, with his fingers on her forehead, is where she'll die.

The digits spread and grip the troughs of her temples. He lifts now, raises her through the clear cement, pulls her right out of the paste, withdraws and leaves her standing, blood-drenched but breathing anew on the firm surface.

The quietness is astonishing, the full softness of silence. Then just a whirr, just the easy noise of the endless hotel, the worded concrete behind the alien man running at impossible speed into the core of the world, images from each window unspooling like film.

It moves a thousand miles a second, yet she has such hyperawareness that it's slowed right down and she can read it all. And the man is weeping, glinting tears on his bright face and the sun is sparkling all over him and it's dazzling beautifully now.

People in the windows are quiet, holding their small machines and sending words outside. Their every letter sticks to the walls for her to know.

And a window passes and inside that room someone holds a little machine unlike the other machines. Inside there a woman clutches a gun and has it pointed at her head and she is saying 'hang for you' and the words stick to the building as they leave her and she is smiling at the girl.

The woman falls away as the image is driven into the ground. Then she passes once more, all alive, and says 'hang for you' and falls away again. And she passes again and again and again and the girl thinks how she knows her so well.

The girl looks at her own skin and sees it's like the man's now, a glazed membrane that's warm and well on her muscles.

Twenty-Three

THE funeral takes place on a warm Saturday, gathers some thirty souls.

The chat is of a robust woman, a resilient battler who raised tough kids in a tough time, a tough place.

'Freda was,' the young clergywoman says, 'among the finest of the fine. She faced great difficulties in her life, not least the murder of her son and the murder of her granddaughter. Yet she carried that heavy pain with a dignity befitting a person of her quality and character.

'When I last met her, just after she'd taken a little runway ride in one of the old Spitfires which had so inspired her love of art, she told me she was "as fit as a trout." I can tell you she showed no sign she was about to leave this world for the next.'

I'm sad at her passing and I know it shows because Bet squeezes my hand, tightens around it as if to say she's with me on this, that she understands how much I liked the doughty old bird.

I turn to Bet, all in black with the blonde hair and blood-red clip, and she looks at me and it's good.

Freda's death was an odd one, has been of curiosity to journalists and tweeters, to politicians and gossipers. She died in custody, died in a car while under arrest, while en route from New Ready House to a police facility in central Belfast.

Her last act had been to visit her locked away great-granddaughter, to see her one final time, perhaps to make whatever peace she could with a girl so alienated by her own family, to claim for whatever reason that she was the troubled young girl's mother.

I don't know how it came to be that she gave the client of New Ready House her cardigan and hat, how it happened that Mim was able to stand up and walk into the world, but that's what occurred.

No authority or state knows what went on from there. They don't know how Mim made it as far as Quarrel Bay on a mission to take her own life, but they know it was fortunate that her decision had been considered by those who knew her best. She had been found in time by her stepfather.

It's been ten days since all of that and no one at all seems to know Mim's biological father lies rotting in his bed, his wife fading away in a room below. Yet nothing is drawing me back to that place, nothing encouraging me to advise anyone of its story.

We step away from the mourners, walk back to Dr Harriet, who waits hand in hand with Mim.

Harriet says she'll take little Mim back now unless we want her to hang around for a while. I'd ask Mim if I felt I'd get anywhere with the question, but all she's doing is looking at us, at Bet, at Harriet, at me, and saying her bits and pieces quietly into herself.

'*...brackets cheaper in the long run with our new free app and steins of beer plus god will be Freda the oldest...*'

I walk closer to her, embrace, feel her hug back, feel how we can both find room among words and noise for this connection.

She looks up and I say, 'We good? We're all good, aren't we Mim?'

And she's all sunburned eyes and going, '*...four oceans change lettings golf cart parked at cooper where OMG save for the scoundrels and please find enclosed...*'

Did She See You?

Says Harriet, 'I'll consider signing her out for an hour with you next Thursday, Denis. But obviously the suicide attempt has complicated things a little.'

'Yeah, I understand. Whatever you decide, Harriet. Thanks.'

She goes, 'Let me know the location in advance. Usual red tape for trips out. Two New Ready House staff must accompany and stay nearby as you meet. Don't think about taking her near any water, by the way.'

So far, as part of the same scheme over recent months, Mim's been escorted by two staff to meet me at my office, at a couple of coffee shops. Among that light-touch, discreet guarding, she's joined me at an HWKC Roundly coaching event in the Waterfront Hall too. Radical immersion treatment, Harriet has called it.

I've told her how I think it's been some kind of therapy for all of us and told her too that I can't say I was entirely present for all of the meetings, in the cerebral sense. The truth is, I can't say I've always been entirely well on those particular days, that my memories are not as clear as they could be, that my imagination seems to have run a little wild on those days.

I learned that about myself at Quarrel Bay. I knew it when Bet arrived, her car scattering sand as she leapt out, raced to where a man and a girl were drowning. I knew it when she pulled Mim and I to shore, when she said amid the kiss of life how, at the bottom of that tree, she looked but could see no girl in the branches, how she had found no such person as Dagny O'Reilly on the internet.

She'd told me as she pumped our hearts that the star of which I had talked had been some anti-version of a girl I knew, that my head had flipped unconnected dead ends, reworked the blandest of words, the blankest of faces, turned it all into a living lie. I know now that I sat with Mim when I sat with Dagny, that I understood Mim when I understood Dagny. I understand now that I've lived the same life as Fiz, that I've been as undone as she became, that in her final days she'd been as undone as I have become.

As Harriet and Mim walk away I wonder now too if Our Trouble might have somehow joined me on a trip I know I planned to make with her once, a little jaunt to see some political murals near a house where I once lodged for a while, where I knew a guy I grew to dislike called Raymond, but my memory's vague. And, anyway, there's no record of such an event so I dismiss it from my mind. I think it's best that way.

Bet drives and says we must stay in business, must keep telling the world love is coming back because that's our journey now. She says it's funny how death makes people think about love, that the guilt she carried from her disconnected husband's suicide had led her to think of ways to connect with others.

She's arranging treatment, she says. She's getting me the support I need just so I can get my head all back together once more, deal with the trauma, make my response to it less theatrical, less debilitating. She's like Fiz when she says she wants to keep me focused only on reality, that I should get stuck into writing that book about the stories we tell ourselves, how it'll be good for our business.

I know I'll make the story right in the book, that it'll be as honest as it can be. It won't include the lies I'd been trying out, the invented forever insult about Mim's constitutional vileness, those attention-grabbing untruths.

Did She See You?

I'll figure out how best to be honest, how to respect her in my story, even though it makes no difference to her, to the world.

I look at Bet, say, 'Thanks.'

She goes, 'Why?'

I say for being there when it counted, for being the fellow sea swimmer I needed, for saving us all.

***

Acknowledgements

Deep thanks to anyone who reads this or any of my writing, and wealth and joy to anyone who comes back for more.

Same goes for anyone who has ever reviewed any of my stuff, but not if they said it was shit.

Heartfelt thanks to my incisive agent Paul Feldstein, who once again knew what to do.

And the same to the one and only Sean for the wordings, and the one and only Jessie for the cover picture.

Printed in Great Britain
by Amazon